WOMAN IN A SPECIAL HOUSE

and other stories

Woman in a Special House

and other stories

Geraldine Clinton Little

FITHIAN PRESS
SANTA BARBARA, 1997

Thanks to the following publications for permission to reprint:

Nimrod for "A Summer Afternoon," finalist in the Katherine Anne Porter Contest.

The DeKalb Literary Arts Journal for "Minister's Wife."

In a Nutshell for "A Clutch of Feathers."

The P.E.N. Syndicated Short Fiction Project for "Reaching for Daisies," under whose auspices, as a prizewinner, it was published in several papers.

Footwork for "Journal."

Mississippi Valley Review for "The Tablecloth."

CrazyQuilt for "The Visitor."

U.S. #1 Worksheets for "Woman in a Special House."

Eight of these stories won the CrazyQuilt First National Fiction Chapbook Contest and were published by CrazyQuilt under the title *Ministries*.

Thanks, too, is extended to the New Jersey Council on the Arts for a grant which made possible the writing of these stories.

The poem quoted in "The Visitor" is "Birago Diop," translated by J. Jahn, London, 1961.

Published by Fithian Press
A division of Daniel and Daniel, Publishers, Inc.
Post Office Box 1525
Santa Barbara, CA 93102

Design by Eric Larson

LIBRARY OF CONGRESS CATALOGING-IN-PUBLICATION DATA
Little, Geraldine Clinton.
    Woman in a special house : and other stories / by Geraldine C. Little.
        p. cm.
     ISBN 1-56474-196-6 (alk. paper)
     I. Title.
  PS3562.I7828W66 1997
  813'.54—dc20   96-9812
                                CIP

Always, for my family

Contents

A Summer Afternoon

"I would have preferred scones," the Reverend Alexander Moore stated with authority to his wife, who had just handed him a thick slice of Irish soda bread heaped with gooseberry jam.

"They're no good cold, Alex, you know that. The bread's fresh. Made just before we left." Margaret Moore, a shy, brown wren of a woman, was almost apologetic. "It's your favorite jam," she added hopefully.

"Mm—and very good it is, too."

Margaret's held breath began again. She had so been afraid of an explosion of temperament, of which the Reverend was brim full.

"I do love a picnic, an afternoon in the open air. There's nothing like it." Alex stretched the six feet two inches of him on a spread car blanket over which Margaret, his Meg, had laid a white cloth and mounds of picnic fare. Leaning on one elbow, Alex held a cup of strong tea ("I like the spoon to almost stand up in it, Meg, you *know* that.") in one hand, the slab of bread on a plate before him. His almost black eyes looked out over the creek where they often came in summer, Alex, Meg, and their two daughters, for a picnic and a swim. It was free, a consideration which was constant in the lives of the Moores.

"It's lovely, dear." Meg busied herself with unpacking the home-grown tomatoes her husband loved. Where was the salt? Hard-boiled eggs. Homemade lemon tarts. Meg always had to get the provender together in short order.

After a morning of visitation on a fine summer day, Alex would come home on the upswing end of his mood cycle and call, "Moira, Ethna. What about going to the creek for a picnic? Meg? Is there any food?"

And of course there was, for Meg baked fresh soda bread daily, as her mother had done all Meg's growing years in Portstewart on the northern coast of Ireland.

Tomatoes sang on the vine, mouth-ready. They were Alex's "gardening." He was Stentorian proud of the few vines which gave them fresh red rounds throughout the summer. When guests came to Sunday tea, a custom kept from European days, Alex shamelessly extolled his prowess with tomatoes. "Love apples, you know. More tea, Miss Greenwood?"

Meg cared for the rest of the garden, quietly.

While the others were gathering fishing equipment: ("Where *is* my tackle box, Meg?" "In the shed by the washer, dear." *Where you left it,* Meg never said aloud), Meg made delectable lemon tarts in minutes, and hard-boiled eggs. The girls piled into a large hamper silverware, china plates, and cups. Alex could not abide paperware. "Poor weak instruments, a curse of the devil, soggy and tinting everything with the taste of cardboard." So Meg brought linen napkins from her mother's chest, a nostalgic legacy, pristine and crisp in silver napkin rings three generations old.

Moira slipped a napkin ("Mama called them serviettes, Moira," Meg had once mused) from her ring, slapdash wiped her mouth, and said to Ethna, "What about a walk through the trees?" At twelve, Moira had learned to say nothing before her father that was not bland, nothing that could be taken issue with. Which was quite brilliant of her, given Alexander Moore's lawyer-like techniques on any, on every, question or statement.

Ethna, ten, not yet so sophisticated in the way of "handling Father," was about to say, "But I'd rather walk to the rope swing." Moira quickly said, "Come, I'll make you a clover chain. You'll be Miriam-who-watched-Moses, and I'll be one of the serving women."

Ethna rose to this with delight. "Oh I'd *love* to be Miriam." She swallowed the last of her tangy tart and followed her sister. "Will you make me a bracelet, too, Moira?"

"Yes, and ankle bracelets if you want them." Moira tried to keep impatience from her voice. *Let's get away from them. Let's go where we can breathe.*

"That's mildly blasphemous, Moira. I doubt that Miriam wore such baubles," Alexander looked up from his job of inspecting fish-hooks.

"Of course you are right, Dada," Moira said, "but since they're flowers of the field, I think God won't mind."

Moira would go far.

"Mm. I suppose not. Be careful, then. Ach, my reel's stuck." He shook the offending reel. Under cover of that distraction, Moira and Ethna left the stretch of cleared bank where they were picnicking and slipped into the wood that bordered the creek.

This was what they loved, this bower they felt was their own. Oaks, older than anyone could imagine, lay on a wonderfully blue sky (had it really always been so blue? Moira was to wonder in after years). There were never clouds. No, there were not. Birds somersaulted and cartwheeled through the trees and tangled vines, the while singing, a feat the girls thought miraculous. Which it was.

They wore nothing but bathing suits. Everyone put on bathing suits at home before leaving, and slipped easy clothes over the suits for quick doffing when they arrived at the picnic site. A paper bag held underwear for going home.

They all loved the water. Dada was a great swimmer, had won races in his youth round the cold headland waters of Ireland. Meg "bathed." She had never learned to swim, a defect of character which Alex tried always to correct.

"Just come as far as my hand," he'd say, going out beyond the small rock-enclosed shallow area where Meg felt safe. But she could not, the only thing she would not do for her husband, her only mild disobedience. She dipped up and down, happy in safe water.

Disgusted, Dada, in earlier years, turned to the girls. His method of getting them to swim was to carry them to the top of the "diving" rock and simply toss them into deep water.

"It's a natural instinct, girls," he had said before the first toss. "No one teaches dogs to swim; they simply do. So will you."

"Mama doesn't," Ethna pointed out before she had learned better.

That brought down a ten-minute sermon and made Mama so miserable that Ethna wanted to cry. Only Moira's hand strongly squeezing hers kept her from making things worse, which would have meant another sermon.

So they were thrown in.

"Wasn't it terrible, terrible, Moira?" Ethna whispered to her sister later when they were alone. "The whole creek in my mouth, the weeds...."

"It was terrible," Moira said in her determined way. "And unforgivable of Dada. We could have drowned, as indeed I thought I was going to. The awful choking, the gasping at nothing, the current dragging me on."

Ethna *did* cry then. The tears of relief, tears of rage. Tears of desperation.

But they learned to swim. Well. Strongly. It left Moira with ambivalent, half-frightened feelings about Alexander Moore's God that they did not develop impossible trauma from the experience. For they did not. Both were to swim, loving it, to the end of their lives. Moira felt, finally, it had more to do with Dada's will than God's.

Now twigs and vines brushed their tanned skin as they wound through the trail they knew to, of course, the bank where the rope swing hung over a sun-touched stretch of the creek.

"You must never tell Dada that we come here," Moira chastised her sister as they looked at the knotted end swaying slightly in an infinitesimal breeze.

"Why not? He loves us to swim." Ethna's eyes, like the color of blown grasses, widened.

"He does *not* like us to swing on the rope. Don't you re-member how he raged after he saved that boy on the far creek last year? No, I forgot. You weren't there."

"I was sick." Ethna remembered the fevered dreams, the sweated sheets.

12

"Well. The boy and his family picnicked near us. The rope swing hung nearby. He shinnied up it and worked himself into a fine motion. He dropped off into a rock half in the water. He was out *cold*," Moira related with delight.

"Oh Moira, did he die?"

"No. He slid away under the water and Dada rescued him, gave him mouth-to-mouth, which was *quite* horrid, and the boy gasped like a fish and was all right. Wasn't he stupid to drop on a rock?"

"Surely he didn't mean to, Moira." Ethna scanned the water under *their* rope swing. There were some rocks at the shoreline.

"Of course not, silly, but he ought to have taken more care." Moira would have been appalled had anyone told her she sounded rather like her father. "So Dada said that day that we were never ever to go on a rope swing." Moira stared at the long twisted thing someone—who?—had attached to a limb of oak.

"Then why—why do we?" Ethna ventured.

Moira turned to her young sister. "Because, my dear, we are *not* silly or careless, and because—it's marvelous fun!" Moira raced to the rope and began to shinny up it.

She did this more easily than Ethna, but still it wasn't easy. The hemp was rough. It was like nettles pricking her. Sometimes she slipped a bit. Her hands reddened, ripped. Once, the rope had rubbed the patch of herself between her legs. The sensation that overtook her was ecstasy; the little clitoris throbbed, throbbed. Moira had almost fallen. That had never occurred again, however much she tried to recapture, to duplicate the maneuvers that led to it.

At last she reached the top. She could stretch out, if she dared loose one hand from the rope, and touch the oak limb holding the rope.

Moira stared down, down at the muddied mirror beneath her. It held everything; it held the world. Look, a bird drifted into a stand of pines. There was another rope, rippled and shadowy. There was a girl on the rope and where would she fall to? Into the sky-that-was-always blue?

Moira called to her sister, who pulled the rope back towards shore, suddenly let it go.

"'How would you like to go up in a swing?'" Moira sang to a curious crow.

Back, forth.

Then she let go. Oh, there was nothing like it. She was a bird, or a butterfly. She existed only in air. She was free of her body, her bones, her burden of sermons and don'ts and God.

The cold creek water opened its arms to her. The shock was a kaleidoscope of delight, like a wanted explosion in her head. Mauve, greens never seen before, a burst of pinky-beige, a shout of blue.

She opened her eyes in the muddy depths. She had not touched bottom but a world of weeds that kissed her legs eerily. There were bubbles. *Why* were there bubbles? The bubbles were magical balls of rainbow. Her hair plumed, danced around her, lashing her face, wandering away as if in wind. She was light, light. All ways were light.

Moira popped through the creek's skin, gasping, laughing. She waved to Ethna, whose hand was at her mouth shaped like an O. Moira floated a moment, to catch her breath. She watched the sky with its furniture of trees, birds. If God lived in that splendid house, why did He thunder so? Why wasn't He happier?

"Moira, come on, swing *me*," Ethna called. Moira sighed, swam to shore, picked her way through pebbles and mud at the edge.

"It's wonderful, wonderful, Ethna. It's the world. Here. I'll hold the rope steady while you go."

Up the rope, fall away to the kingdom of water and sky in that water, breath leaping, the heart dancing. Over and over again. Until they were exhausted.

They lay on a patch of weedy grass, silent, filled.

"I'll make you a crown," Moira said suddenly, out of the silence. "And bracelets."

"Yes, you'd better, or Dada will ask questions."

"We could tell him we threw them away."

"We could, but that would be a lie, Moira."

Moira looked at her young sister. "Yes, so it would." She began to fashion jewels of clover, making a hole in the stem of one, carefully, carefully, so it didn't rip. As carefully, she pulled the stem of another clover through the little hole until the flowerhead stopped its passage.

"Would you like to have been Miriam?" Ethna asked when, gemmed, she stood by a birch, touching her crown.

Moira considered. "No. I'd rather be the Egyptian Princess. But, Ethna, suppose Miriam hadn't watched Moses. Suppose there had been a rope swing strung up near the bulrushes and she climbed up it and fell away into another world. Suppose *that*, Ethna. Where would Moses be?"

Ethna thought. "In Egypt, wouldn't he?"

"No," said Miriam. "He would *not*. He would have drifted away on the stream, away, away to the ocean. Why, he might have drifted to *Ireland*, Ethna, and lived with kings of Ireland. You're Ethna/Miriam, Princess of Ireland." Moira laughed, scooped water from the creek and put it on her sister's head. "There, I've christened you, Princess Ethna."

"Oh Moira," Ethna laughed, too. The birches and oaks trembled with laughter. The rocks clapped their hands and the green weedy earth chuckled.

"What about God?" Ethna asked, suddenly.

"What *about* God?" Moira frowned.

"He wouldn't have allowed that, you know. Why, you've changed the *Bible*, Moira."

"So I have." Moira scribbled in the dirt with a stick.

Ethna shivered. "We must go back, Moira, the sun's going down. Dada will be furious with us." She tore off the crown, the wrist and ankle bracelets as if they burned her. "Come on, Moira, come *on*."

Moira lingered at the creek edge for a moment. She looked up at the rope just barely swaying. She looked at the water beneath, and the sky above.

"It's the time in the air that's the best," she said aloud. "After you let go of the rope, before you enter the water. *That's* the best time."

Moira turned and went after her sister through the wood.

She noticed a few leaves turning blood red. Autumn was near, and after it, winter. She saw the rope hanging, snow-whitened over iced water.

But the air would be there, waiting.

Yes.

She gathered up the innocence of her summer face, an offering to her father.

The Tablecloth

"But it's threadbare, Mom. Even has a hole at one end. Why don't you throw it away? What'll my friends think?"

Noreen is sixteen. It is June of her junior year in high school. Three friends are coming for an end-of-the-school-year luncheon party and a swim.

"When we were at Edna's everything was perfect. Green tablecloth and pink roses, even the china had roses...." Noreen's voice trails off; she goes out to gather flowers. Nothing must be different; similarity to one's peers is *everything*.

Noreen is right. The cloth *is* threadbare. But very beautiful, in the way of an ancient painting in need of cleaning.

Mary Simpson stares at the Irish linen cloth which was her grandmother's. It once was whitest white. It is now a yellowing ivory. Where it is wearing thin, the tiny threads, like a carefully made web, are visible. The small hole (at an end which would hang down below the edge of the table, hardly visible) is like a small window, a peephole to unraveling time.

She folds the cloth. The hole is uppermost. *Why don't you throw it away?* The cloth is useless. Even if the hole were repaired by invisible mending, it is clear other holes will soon appear, the tiny threads will give up their hold on the twisting, impossible, often miraculous stories breathed over them.

Mary takes the cloth towards the light dawdling in through the bay window. Noreen is just disappearing down a lane of daylilies flame-colored and still in the quiet air.

Sunlight burns right through the hole. The window widens.

Louisa was Mary's grandmother. Louisa is visiting a farm, Black Ditch, in the purple/azure hills of Wicklow. She has

17

been sent there for the summer. In her family are ten children and little money. Her aunt and uncle have agreed to keep Louisa "until you and Donald find two coins to rub together." The aunt, Mrs. Maureen Clarke (she never calls herself, or thinks of herself, as Mrs. James Clarke), sniffs. It is evident she thinks no such coins will ever exist. She is right.

Louisa, tall, with black curls tumbling down her back, sits on a stool beside a stout woman swathed in a voluminous apron.

"You can't strip it, surely, Fannie. Oh the poor thing." Louisa's eyes are riveted on the chicken the servant, Fannie, holds between her knees.

"Sure it's dead, child. Did you not see me wring its neck? It can't feel anything." Strong hands begin to pluck feathers from the limp fowl.

Louisa sucks in her breath. She is sure that, even dead, *she* would know if someone were pulling the tiny hairs from her skin. She did watch the neck wringing, an act performed so fast she almost didn't know it had happened, though she was thrilled almost to vomiting.

She shudders now, wants to look away. Fascinated, she can't take her eyes off the fleet hands, the flying feathers.

She is pretty in the dark Spanish way of many Irish. She is talented on the piano. Mrs. Clarke feels something may be made of her. She feels it is her mission in life, at least for this summer, to be the instrument of that making. She has a splendid pump organ (no one plays it) at one end of the parlor, and a fairly passable spinet at the other. Her home is ponderously genteel. Mr. Clarke's farm has done very well. They have no children of their own.

"Why couldn't they have taken *four* of ours for the summer, all that room, fields and the cattle to be worked. The boys would have been fine help," Louisa's mother says to her husband the evening Aunt Maureen's letter comes by the late post. The children have gone to bed; the lamp is about to be blown out in their bedroom.

"She couldn't have stood the boys, my love. Maureen's delicate, you know. Let us be grateful for what she has done,

18

though I'll miss Louisa." He thinks of Louisa singing to him as he slops the pigs, helping him when she can. Louisa down on hands and knees in the grass, staring a long time at wild primroses.

"Delicate, my foot," Anna Corr, a small, energetic woman remarkably slim despite (because of?) her progeny, blows out the lamp with angry breath. "Strong as one of her own bulls, Maureen is. The two of them rattling in that big farmhouse. And as for grateful, Donald Corr, I wonder at you. Aren't they the lucky ones to have our Louisa to spark evenings when the two of them, speechless as stuffed magpies, stare at each other in that overflowing parlor?"

"Aye. Lucky indeed." Donald sighs, turns over as his wife climbs into the high bed, thumps bolster and pillow, and shortly begins to snore. He lies a long time in the moonless room, black as potatoes in his souring fields.

"It'll be grand, stewed for dinner," Fannie pats the chicken, not quite so plump as when in its white finery. "Pick up those feathers, child."

"We'll never eat it!" Louisa's hand flies to her mouth.

"And why not? What on earth way were you brought up? Did your dad never strip a chicken, and him with all those young ones to feed?"

"We—we—I never saw him do it." Louisa can't say that her father, with an innate sensitivity, would take the chickens out behind the barn and never allow Louisa to be there when he had to kill one.

"You'll be soon enough acquainted with death," he'd said, once, when Louisa asked him where he was taking a squawking fowl from the frantic barnyard. She never asked again, for he had seemed so sad, his face suddenly like a strong plant withered.

"Daft, *I* say," Fannie waddles off, the chicken tucked under her fat arm.

What Louisa loves is the field of flax, oh, a very small field at the back of her uncle's farm. She roams there, when she can, among the pert green leaves, the white and blue flowers—so symmetrical! She took one, blue as the sky, and sat with it on a boulder, one day, delighted with its perfection. Five sepals, five petals, ten stamens, she remembers a bit of botany learned in school.

"Pretty enough, child, but nothing special," Aunt Maureen says briskly that evening at supper when Louisa animatedly talks of the flower.

Nothing special? The blue of it, like holding a piece of heaven, the perfect parts, wasn't it a piece of God?

"It's made into linen, of course. The cloth we're dining on." Aunt Maureen never said "eating on."

They were sitting in a long, somewhat narrow dining room with windows that looked out to a garden of multi-colored lupins and, beyond, the hills. The table was immense for three people.

"Missus never wants the three leaves taken out," Fannie said one day when Louisa asked why it was kept so long. "It's grander large, y'see."

How cold grandness is: Louisa thinks of the small table at home, its homespun rough cloth, the bubbling talk around it, Alex, her brother, nudging her to move her elbow, please, or he'll eat it for certain, everyone laughing, telling jokes, talking over each other, her mother making bread and milk do, again, for the lot of them.

When will the trees begin to change color, the fields to sway in a crisper breeze, so she can go home?

Tonight she looks down at the cloth, smooth and shining, white as a summer cloud. How lovely it is, with Aunt Maureen's tall golden (brass, she is to learn later) candlesticks holding pale white candles dropping patterned shadows on it. It is, she thinks, like eating in that field full of the perfectly made flowers, listening to the small tinkle of them in the summer breeze, saffron-colored butterflies dizzy over them.

"How—festive—to eat on *this* every night," Louisa's eyes shine towards her straight-backed aunt now pouring tea from a silver pot.

"It's what your mother was used to," Aunt Maureen frowns, "until she married *him*. You ought to learn what it is like." Her voice is as dark as tea without milk. "After supper you will play one tune for us, Louisa," Maureen rushes on without giving the girl a chance to reply to the mystery of that "him." "Then we must go to bed. This is an early-rising household."

It was. Uncle Jim to his farm chores, Aunt Maureen to the endless overseeing of the household and farm accounts. It is Aunt Maureen who sees that the books work in their favor. She likes, too, to smooth (iron) the linen tablecloths herself. "They're done right if *I* do them," she'd say, out of Fannie's hearing. Sometimes in it. Fannie simply scowls.

So in the long Irish twilight Louisa plays the intricacies, the wild forests and silken coverlets of Chopin's "Fantasie Impromptu," for Louisa is to go on to play on the concert stage, in America, until marriage and children turn her fingers to common tasks, the simpler melodies of dailiness.

At the end of August, when the flax is almost ready to be gathered, put into stacks for drying, when the hills take on tones of russet and maroon, when Louisa has learned to eat Fannie's plucked chickens with only an inward flinching, when the long summer evenings shorten, it is time to go back in the trap, with her boxes and cases. Back home.

"I have put a linen cloth, the one you liked, in the bottom of your case, Louisa, my dear." Austere Maureen unbends this far. "It will remind you of finer things when—" She breaks off. "No matter. It is *yours*, mind. It is not to be used by the crowd of you. It is for your wedding chest."

"But—but you will come to my wedding." Louisa, so tall already, bends to kiss her remote aunt.

"The dear Lord knows about *that*. I want you to have it now. Go on now, Jim. It's a long journey."

"Three hours will do it." Uncle Jim helps Louisa up and folds up the little step, slaps the chestnut-colored horse, and they are off.

Aunt Maureen waves a linen handkerchief after them.

Louisa waves back until the rigid figure becomes a speck against the dwindling whitewashed farmhouse, the diminishing trees, the gentle hills.

She never saw Aunt Maureen again; Maureen died the following year.

"Heart—or lack of it," Louisa's mother murmurs over Uncle Jim's laboriously written letter.

That night Louisa dreams of the fertile black loam of Black Ditch, two golden candlesticks with lighted tapers glimmering over it.

Louisa, old, lives with Mary and Mary's parents, has done so all Mary's growing-up years. Like most old people, Louisa likes to tell stories. Mary, at sixteen—just Noreen's age now—is mostly annoyed by the long, meandering histories of people she has never known, will never know.

She will have to be the mother of Noreen before she understands this source, as of a river endlessly spilling across pebbled bottoms, which spills to the tributary of Noreen.

It is in America that Mary hears of the cloth, the summer at Black Ditch, Fannie, and the marvel of perfect flax flowers. The one story, out of the endless trickle of Louisa's tongue, she likes to hear, over and over again, is of the Black Ditch summer.

"How *dreadful* that you could eat those chickens, Grannie," Mary always says. "I couldn't do that."

"You could if you were good and hungry," Louisa laughs. "Aunt Maureen didn't serve joints or cutlets often, for they did strange things to Uncle Jim's digestion. Stewed chicken he would have eaten, day after day, and almost did, day after day."

"And the flowers, tell me about the flax, I've never seen it growing."

"Of course you haven't, more's the pity. Why would you?" And Mary, who slept in the same room as her grandmother Louisa, for lack of space (like Louisa's mother, Mary's mother had many children), would feel soft Irish rain on her cheeks at dusk, would see the white-and-blue flowers, like gem chips, and a lonely girl wandering through the field.

When Grannie Louisa died, the linen cloth was labeled "For Mary," in Grannie's quavery handwriting.

Mary puts the cloth over her arm. (She will get out the crocus-yellow cloth for Noreen's party, with the pale green glass plates.) She walks upstairs to her old chest, Louisa's wedding chest, brought into the clamor of Ellis Island, then to the strange attic room of a daughter's small house, and, at last, here, to Mary's suburban split-level home with a swimming pool in the backyard.

Carefully, she wraps the cloth in tissue paper and puts it in the chest, labeling it "For Noreen."

Will Noreen throw it out? Or will its threads of history tether her as they have tethered Mary, who, standing over the closed chest, remembers, suddenly, sharply, the intense dislike, the churning anger carefully hidden, that she felt when her grandmother, Louisa, in the middle of the night got up to use the bathroom, the flapping combinations always worn at night wafting odors of the aged towards her, Mary, young as a new stalk of flax, the field of the whole world ahead of her who would never, never be old.

Shall a Little
Child Lead Them?

The horse trough lies at the foot of a small hill, on the left-hand side of trolley tracks that, a few feet beyond the trough, loop round an ancient shed, now an office and coffee shop, for the return trip back to the city. The trough is a large oval, made of stone hewn out of the quarry that lies gaping up at the top of Chestnut Hill, far beyond where the trolley runs. The back of the trough is actually a high wall, from which a horse's carved head stares, its open mouth empty of the water that used to spew forth into the basin below. In the days when horses used the trough, perhaps as many as five at once could have dipped thirsty mouths to its offered relief.

The small girl now sitting on the edge of the stone basin likes to come here. For one thing, it is at the entrance to Valley Green, that lovely park whose winding paths lead this way, that way, for hikers, and whose bridle paths still are ways of peace in a dissonant world.

Ellen, for that is the little girl's name, likes to imagine that the trough is still full of water, likes to conjure up the figure of a horse or two—white, brown, nostrils flaring— about to dip noble heads to the water. Sometimes she sees carriages affixed to the horses, sometimes just a single rider who sits, while the horse drinks, looking into Valley Green's leafy entrance, impatient to get going. Sometimes she peoples the carriages. Whether in carriages or on horses, her people are always in old-fashioned dress. The ladies, if they are on the horses of her imagination, wear long skirts and sit decorously side-saddle. If they are in the carriages, they peer curiously out of green-curtained windows as if waiting for life to begin.

25

The men are always tall, handsome, and moustached. Sometimes they wear high hats, sometimes brisk caps. They always wear red coats, the kind of costume she pores over in books at home of "The Hunt," which lie on her mother's coffee table. Her mother does not hunt now; she was injured in a fall some years before. She talks glowingly to her small daughter of the heady delights of hearing the starting horn, of racing through brilliant countrysides after a tiny (and defenseless) creature, of champagne afterwards among braced-up people.

It is autumn now; the countryside is vivid with color. Many leaves have already fallen so that the old trough, shadowed with maple trees, bubbles (Ellen's word) with yellows, oranges, maroons, and browns, like a magic water, pushed to and fro by a brisk wind.

Ellen picks up a stick, a small branch of a maple. She turns to the trough, dangling her feet into the "water." She begins to stir the leaves, liking the crackling, whispering sound they make.

Intrigued, she slides off the basin's side right into the trough, walks towards the back wall, gently swishing her stick. It is, in her mind, a rider's crop.

"Hey—what—" a voice swims up from a deep pile of leaves. A man sits up, rubbing dust from his eyes.

"Eeee," Ellen screams, retreats a little, but comes back, slowly, for the man is putting on a high hat—oh, somewhat battered and dirty, but nevertheless a genuine high hat such as she has seen in pictures in the books at home.

"Are—are you a rider?" she ventures, looking curiously at the man.

"Rider?" His voice is gravelly, as if it were full of leaves that irritate. "Rode that trolley couple days ago. Last buck I had. Found this place to sleep. Pretty warm under the leaves."

"You *slept* here?" Ellen is entranced. What fun to sleep in the horse trough under the colored water.

"Got nowhere else. It's better than the city street, fifty ways better than the shelter. They stole all my stuff there."

Ellen was puzzled. "Shelter? You mean your home? Your

family stole your stuff?"

"Haven't any family" he muttered. "Haven't any home. You got any money?" he asked, looking at Ellen's good jeans, her fine-combed cotton blouse, her cashmere sweater.

"No home! That's terrible. *Everybody* has a home, you know."

"What grade you in, little girl?"

"Second. I should be there today, but I'm—I—wanted to come to the horse trough. It's such a shiny day; you shouldn't waste shiny days, should you? You won't tell, will you?" Ellen frowns at the man.

"Who'd I tell? You got any money?" he repeats.

Ellen feels in her jeans pockets. "I have two dollars. Why? You want to take the trolley again?"

"No way. Not goin' back into the city. I like it out here. Maybe I'll go on into that park for the winter."

"You mean," Ellen comes a little nearer to the man, "you're going to spend the *whole* winter in Valley Green Park?"

"That the name of it? Who cares. Maybe. Except nobody'll give me any money or food in there, I guess."

"Well," Ellen thought for a moment. "Far down in the park there's the Inn, you know. Mom and Dad take me there sometimes. You could buy food there."

"*Buy* food!" The man's laugh is not pleasant. "Kid, you don't understand. I don't have money for food, I don't have any home, I don't have any family."

"But—but *everyone* has a home." The conversation seemed to have come full circle.

"Don't teach you much in second grade, do they."

"I don't know," says Ellen, worried. "I've only been there a month."

"Never heard of street people?"

"I've heard of street *cleaners*." Ellen remembers a scene in her reader.

"Not the same thing at all. We're part of what street cleaners *clean*." He brushes leaves off his shoulder.

"Want some of my lunch?" Ellen is mystified, but she

points to her lunch pail, back on the basin rim where she left it.

"What d'you have?" He stands up, a tall man, Ellen sees with delight. In her imagination the People of the Trough are always tall.

"I don't know. Mom always surprises me. Come on and see." She wades back to the rim, sits and opens her pail. It is green, painted with a tawny horse's head.

The man moves, fast as he can, to her side.

"A sandwich," Ellen announces. "Looks like cheddar cheese and sliced ham, which I love, loaded with mustard. A big, fat sandwich. Hmm—an apple and a package of three chocolate Tastycakes." She beams at him. "Pretty good, huh? Here. Take half the sandwich."

He stares at the food before grabbing it. Then he stuffs it into his mouth, almost in one bite.

"Wow, you'll be sick if you eat *that* fast." She is still deliberately chewing her half.

"Can I—you gonna share the cakes?"

"Course. I can't eat all three. I sometimes swap with Nancy King. She brings little pies, some days." Ellen carefully unwraps the package, hands the man two cakes. "I only want one. Mom made me a great big breakfast this morning."

He takes the cakes without a word, begins again to stuff them into his mouth, his eyes, the while, on the apple.

"If you slept here," Ellen begins between bites of her cake, "what'd you have for breakfast?"

"Didn't have any."

"Goodness. No wonder you're so hungry. Here, take the apple. We've got a whole basket of them at home; I love to have one when I get home from school."

School. Ellen looks a bit uneasy. Will they call home?

"Wouldn't want to buy me a cup of coffee, would ya?" The man wipes his mouth with the back of his hand.

"Oh—there's milk in my thermos, but—well, sure. There's a little store at one end of that shed over there. I better not come in with you, though. They might—might tell someone I'm not in school."

28

He looks at her. "You could just give me the two dollars and I'll go over there myself while you have your milk."

"That's a good idea," she smiles at him, fishes deep in her pocket for two bills. "Will you come back? I'm going to stay here all afternoon." *Until school is out,* she does not say.

"Sure, yeah, I'll be back." He takes the bills fast, looking around him. Nope, nobody watching. He shuffles to the curb, leaves falling from him as from a shaggy tree. He waits for a break in the traffic flow (not much at this hour), and makes for the back of the shed where the coffee shop plies its trade mostly for the trolley men who stop there before looping back to the city.

She watches him disappear into the shop, turns back to her pail, pours her thermos top full of milk.

Mm. A shiny day indeed. A bird slips his quick shadow into her milk, lifts towards the sun. Just beyond the Valley Green entrance, Canada geese squawk skyward, bound for warmer places, she supposes. She watches them. What makes them form a V? She will ask her teacher that. A black cat runs from the sidewalk into the quiet of the park. Leaves sway, talk. Berries wink and glisten in the sunlight.

She finishes her milk, puts the thermos in the pail and closes it with a snap.

She looks towards the shed.

Isn't it time he came back? It's the first time anyone out of her imagination has actually appeared at the trough, let alone *in* it. But, it strikes her, he must live here, that's what he meant. He's one of the people she has always placed here. Did he fall from his horse, like Mom? Where is the horse, then? Trailing away without him down the lanes of Valley Green? She imagines it, white mane streaming in the wind, its hooves flying free and riderless down the long leafy colored lanes, in the shiny autumn air.

She laughs aloud, claps her hands.

And finds he has returned. He sits beside her on the rim.

"Man, that was good." The coffee was fifty cents, second cup free. He doesn't give her back the change.

She grins at him. "Mom won't let me have coffee yet."

"She's right." He stares into the horse trough. "Lots of time for coffee."

"That's what Mom says."

They sit in comfortable silence for a while, shawled in light.

"I love it here," Ellen says, finally.

"Oh, love." He shrugs his shoulders.

"Don't you love it here? You must, to sleep here."

"I sleep here because—" he breaks off. "You oughta go to school, you know."

"Oh, I do, certainly I *do*. It's just today—today. I told you, I didn't want to waste it. You have to save shiny days. Like pennies. Mom puts pennies in a big jar in the kitchen."

"Yeah." He slumps into himself, his high hat at a precarious angle.

"Want to walk a little bit down the park lane?"

He stares at her. "You shouldn't go with strange men like that."

"I know. Mom said. But you're not strange. Why, you're one of the horse trough people."

"You're a strange kid."

"Maybe," she laughs. "C'mon." She jumps up, starts to walk down the lane into the park.

After a moment he follows, slowly. "My legs ain't so good," he mumbles.

But they walk, walk, in the uncommon common autumn afternoon, down to a bend in the lane. Ellen talks, sometimes, to him about her family, about the people of the horse trough, talks sometimes to squirrels that skitter up trees as they near, to birds that whisk into bushes and out, mouths red or blue with berries.

He listens, sometimes murmurs a monosyllable.

"Can't go any further," Ellen says at last, frowning. "Got to get home when school is over. Do you know what time it is?"

He squints at the sky. "Nope, but it's time for you to go, I can tell by the slant of the sun."

"*Can* you?" She stares up at the round orange ball, a hand shading her eyes. "Wish I could do that. But then you're—"

Horse Trough people. Wonderful. "Are you coming back, too?"

"Think I'll go on down round the bend a bit." He stares into the dark overshadowed lanes. *Maybe there's a cave or something, maybe an old shack.*

"Sure. But you'll come back to the horse trough, won't you? To sleep, I mean?"

"Maybe. Maybe I'll just keep on lookin.'"

For his horse. Of course.

"You'll find it," Ellen says, patting his arm.

He stares at her.

"Round the bend. You'll find it. Gotta go. So long; it's been a great, shiny day."

She waves, turns, walks back towards the horse trough, its font of colored water swirling, whispering of days past, and to come.

In the distance a trolley bell clangs as the trolley loops back to the rude, rejecting city.

The Visitor

"He won't come, of course. It's a mad idea, Dr. Knox. No one will be able to understand him." Elder Kruger pulled at his long white beard, his eyes flint-grey in the evening sun. Those eyes were a surprise. You could mistake them for easygoing orbs, unseeing as a hen's in a dusty farmyard, and as stupid. In fact they were hawk's eyes, missing nothing, able to spot a mouse in the dark.

"He *will* come, John," I said. "I've been in touch with him. He's a friend. I can understand a lot of what he says, not well enough for my liking, but I'm getting better all the time at some of the old words he uses. I've found an interpreter who'll explain what's necessary to explain."

"What's the point of it?" Kruger was testy. "We've enough problems here, *real* problems, the natives arrogant and rioting easily as a berry drops from a bush, at *nothing*. It will cost dear to bring him from West Africa; oh they've learned to charge, these fellows."

I slapped down my teacup. "He'll not take anything, John. He'd be insulted if you offered. It's a matter," I glared at the old Elder, "of good will."

"Good will!" Kruger almost spat into the warm South African night. "Good will is to stay where he belongs and not come here stirring up people."

I took a long, long breath. "He's not coming to make a political speech. I told you that, John. He's a griot, a wiseman. He has preserved in his mind hundreds of years of oral history of his village. Think of it!" I imagine, myself, trying to tell anything much of *our* village beyond forty or fifty years past.

"Wiseman, rot. I tell you it'll turn political." Kruger rose, a tall lank figure, like, I always thought, an ancient prophet. Which shows you how deceiving looks can be.

"I give you my word it won't, John. Surely you trust your minister, son of a former minister? You've known us a long time, for my father visited this church."

"I trust *you*, Trevor Knox. Would trust you with anything I have; it's *him* I can't trust. How do you know he won't switch the storytelling to a diatribe?"

"I trust him, just as you trust me." Simply, I did. "He's a *friend*, I keep telling you."

"Fool, then, you, to trust a native. Look at the way they're turning on us who've given them everything, their very lives."

"Yes." I looked out at the dry sandy earth and its stunted karroo bushes, in the distance low hills. Milk bushes with long finger-like leaves were beginning to be touched with light from a full African moon. "Yes," I said softly to a great moth the night had brought forth. "We've given them everything that doesn't matter."

"Law? Order? Not matter? Are you losing your mind, Dr. Knox? Gone soft in the head?" Kruger rapped a black cane on the floor. "Be careful, Doctor. You're spending too much time with those natives. Oh, I know," he raised a hand as I opened my mouth, "you're trying to make peace, you say. All well and good, but," his stern unyielding profile was impressive with the full moon on it, "not peace at any cost. England saw what *that* meant. Good night, Doctor. I hope you—we all—don't regret this insane visit." He sliced his cane through the night air like a sword and tramped off, the moon flashing on his straight back until he was a dot.

I'd been born in Ottoshoop, in Southwest Africa. My father had emigrated from the north of Ireland at the age of twenty-one. We'd little, financially. But I had the open veldt, and horses to ride, early in the freshness of morning and in the evening when the sunset flamed glorious in clear air.

My father had made friends with the griot, a fierce-looking mild man with tales in his head that seemed, to my father, akin to the old tales the storytellers of Ireland spun.

"Aye, the ancients," he'd say, after an evening listening to the griot, "they've the real wisdom; they'll save us all. They came before and will go on after politics."

This before politics became the intense issue they now are.

My father had been moved by the diocese to South Africa, to a missionary church just starting up, before I had the advantage Father had of listening long into the night to ancient tales remarkably told. My father was privileged, the only white man invited to listen. He'd begun to write down some of the old tales, but there was a fire before we moved. Some said it was set by natives who resented any white man listening to a sacred history. I don't know. We never found out who set it. But the written tales perished.

"I'll re-write them," Father said. But he never did. Demands were constant in the new missionary station, and money short, as always.

Two years after his arrival in that place, Father died. A year after that my mother, whom I'd seen, when in West Africa, bake one hundred loaves a day in an outside oven, whom I'd seen kill and cut up sheep for sale, died too, worn but never daunted by the hard, hard life of it all.

I went to seminary back in the north of Ireland. My father's unfinished work was all I wanted to do, *had* to do. Here, in this suburb of Johannesburg.

I never forgot the griot. That was part of Father's unfinished business. I began to work on committees of natives and whites. There was no consistency in the way most of my parishioners thought, and the Christian message I preached. And preaching, I soon found, was miles away from doing any good. Hands on was the only way.

So I met the griot Lokuryamoi again, an old man now, frail as a withered twig, with long white hair and a face lined with rivers like the Transvaal rivers, brown, twisting, laden with a thousand hurts and injustices. He remembered my father. With great affection, he was kind enough to say. He put his arms around me. Yes, he'd come to speak the old tales. Would anyone really be interested? I reassured him on that point, though I myself was unsure. Was I putting him in danger? Had I any right? Had I the right to withhold him? People needed to hear the way the world was before *we* came with our pale skins and insolent voices. I had to take the chance. We all had to take chances. It was the only way.

Early rains had washed away the dust of two dry months when the griot came. There was a freshness in the air.

"If we could have it round a campfire," I'd ventured to my elders that morning, "how authentic it would be."

"Daft is what you are, Reverend." Alex MacKnight, about to leave my study, slammed its door shut. "Isn't it bad enough, any blacks who'll come angry at your presuming on their history, our own congregation angry at your absurd liberal views. In the open, round a campfire...." Alex shuddered. "It's that streak of Irish romanticism in you, Reverend, that too often mists your mind." He said it as if I'd gone whoring. I could always count on Alex for forthrightness. Of course he was right, I suppose.

So the large hall had been set up with hard-backed chairs. "Not the sanctuary. We'll not go that far, Dr. Knox. Who knows *what* he'll preach."

"All right, all right. You *will* not understand that it is history he's telling."

The hall, mostly used for Sunday school, was bleak, dun-colored, in need of repainting. It boasted a small platform at one end which held a lectern and a scratchy public address system, which made me irrationally angry.

"He can't possibly use that thing," I jabbed at Van Koop, one of my board members. "And the lectern—it's ridiculous. He's a *storyteller*. All this technical stuff and formality will dampen his spirit."

Just as well, Van Koop's eyes murmured, but all he said was "It's there if he wants it, Trevor."

I swallowed, hard.

I'd wanted to fetch Lokuryamoi from the west in my old car, but he said no.

"My grandson will bring me, but he will not come into

your meeting. He will wait at the home of his cousin. He knows my needs. And there will be no interpreter. I know your tongue."

He did, of course, somewhat brokenly. But if he wished to speak to us directly, I wanted him to do that. I understood the courtesy of that effort.

I welcomed Lokuryamoi to the platform, and oh, ah, he was fragile. But I would not have dreamt of offering him a hand up the four steps. *That* was one of his needs, that I recognize his dignity, which was immense and flowed out over the restless, mixed audience. For of course he was part of an old magic.

We sat in two carved chairs made of an ancient wood he knew better than I. Had the kings of his country sat in such chairs eons ago? Van Koop was right. I was a romantic Irishman and had better realize that I was responsible for an amazing old man whose safety meant more to me than my own. Was responsible, too, for making this meeting, a meeting in all its meanings, work. I wanted no riot torched by my own hand, which I hoped would be the hand of peace.

I introduced Lokuryamoi, telling of his wisdom, of the oral history preserved in his mind: hundreds of years. Lokuryamoi sat, half smiling at the mostly white faces before him. (The few blacks there were crunched together at the back of the hall.) Lokuryamoi's face was not impassive. It was full of mobility. And humor. And tears.

He rose, exotic in his baboon-skin cape, his long white hair spilling onto the tawny skin, which seemed alive.

He raised a hand, did not smile at the audience. Without a word, he began to push aside the lectern with its mike which falsified. I rushed to help him. In the heat of the hall there was only the scrape and bump of the lectern. Then he began to push his carved chair to the front of the platform. Silently, I helped him center it.

You could feel the spectators' held breath. Would this old, old creature faint from the effort? What on earth was Dr. Knox up to, anyway?

Lukoryamoi sat in the chair, and carefully arranged his

beautiful cape around him. He closed his eyes for a long moment. Then he opened them, dark, wide, deep, and looked over the entire room, slowly, not a corner missed, not a face undiscovered.

And spoke.

"'If your face is ugly, learn to sing.'" He paused. "Now I will chant a song of the earth which sustains us...."

The voice was not fragile; it was strong, pinging to the last row of chairs and beyond, out into the dark, sighing African night. It was as if all the voices of the past lived in him.

It was amazing. Not a performance. Lokuryamoi did not perform, though he knew his worth. He simply spoke the history of his village, his clan. It was a magical world of ritual, dance, masks, and laughter. And troubles. A meeting of matter and spirit which became, were, in fact, one. The cosmos became a sea of fluid forces which perpetually vibrated and manifested themselves in different ways in particular times and places. All of the past were alive: the slaves of his village, the leaders, the gods. And could never be killed.

> *Those who are dead are never gone,*
> *they are in the breast of the woman,*
> *they are in the child who is wailing,*
> *and in the firebrand that flames.*
> *The dead are not under the earth:*
> *they are in the fire that is dying,*
> *they are in the grasses that weep,*
> *they are in the whimpering rocks,*
> *they are in the forest, they are in the house,*
> *the dead are not dead.*

Lokuryamoi's voice did not die away. It ended triumphant, as if trumpets, that we sometimes had for Easter Sunday morning service, were sounding forth full blast.

From that little, ancient, frail griot. The wiseman.

I happened to look out at Kruger, in the terrible, wonderful, full silence absorbing the hall. His jaw had fallen open.

The eyes you could mistake for a hen's were stark, and stared. At the small immense man on the platform. And far beyond. Oh, far beyond.

...they are in the house
the dead are not dead.

The message echoed out into the night full of stars you could almost touch. It wrote itself on thorntree, on each building raised up on this man's earth, on prickly pear trees and silken grasses. It was graven, that night, on sheep kraals and huts, on farmhouses and great castles of the white men. It was written on the moon, who offered only her dark side so that words could be writ large, in flaming letters, and on the spider's web that, everyone knew, was a ladder to the stars. It floated back to us, stunned, with all the stinks, wailings, joys, and unbearable sorrows, that yet were borne, of the past, this present.

I could not possibly tell you how long we sat in that bleak hall, after, buffeted by shadows, the strong enduring shades, before rising to greet Lokuryamoi, the wiseman.

Reaching for Daisies

The postcard no longer exists. Lost in that other time. It is the scene before me this morning that makes me think of it:

Dear Kyoko:
This spot on the seacoast is what we see from our living room window. I run across our rocky field, across a road, and sit on a rock to watch waves crashing against the rocks. When you come, we'll sit there together. (I am cheating. Should be writing this in Japanese, but it's summer and I'm too lazy. Maybe your teacher will help you with it?)
  Your Pen Pal,
  Mona

But I was too stubborn (too shy?) to ask Mr. Amura for help. Besides, he would just have told me it was a fine project for me to work on myself.

"Things we earn we appreciate more."

He was full of proverbs like that. After I read about Benjamin Franklin, I wondered if Mr. Amura had read him and incorporated him into his own system of education.

It took me the whole summer, for I, too, felt lazier when the warm breezes made my kimono feel hot on my legs, when crickets chattered the night away in the grove of pine trees near our house, when, houses open for air, I heard, far into the night, Mrs. Nukada playing her cheap flute.

I propped up the card against a lacquer box on the little desk where I did my schoolwork. Long before I could read Mona's message I had walked into the Maine scene many times. It is of a lake ringed by pine trees. In the foreground great rocks jut into a very blue sky touched here and there with downy clouds. Colorful wildflowers and weeds lap at the base of the rocks. A clump of large white daisies with brilliant orange centers particularly took my fancy. How I wanted to pick them, arrange one or two on one of my mother's handsome trays with a twist of old bark and a few pebbles.

Before I understood what she had written about sitting on one of those immense rocks, that is exactly what I wanted to do. I imagined myself taking pad and brush, clambering past the wildflowers, carefully, carefully, and settling myself on the one that had a flatish surface. Looking down on the surf below, I would capture it on my sketch pad. Perhaps I would even put in the small white sailboat almost out of the picture on the left.

It was quite wonderful. That seacoast, immense, grand, the great rocks like grey gods. So different from the landscape of our inland sea.

By the end of the summer, my fifteenth summer, the summer I discovered that I might be beautiful, a thing I had thought quite impossible, I had the whole card perfectly (I think) translated. I was wild to go to America. Forgetting decorum, I wrote to Mona at the end of September.

> Dear Friend Mona:
> I have worked out all the meaning of your English
> words and I am wild to come to America. I would like
> to see the rocks, the little sailboat, the ivory daisies
> with suns for centers....

I wrote in Japanese. It wasn't meant to be unkind. Or retaliatory. Simply, the wildness tumbled out, like a kite streaming in the wind. I couldn't wait for the restraint of finding the proper English words. It was stupid of me; it would take her a while to translate.

"But I couldn't anyway go to America now, with winter coming on." I laughed at myself in the glass Mama gave me as a birthday present.

I was ashamed for how much time I spent looking at my-self in the glass that fifteenth summer. Suddenly, I had become slim rather than skinny, and had a pleasing roundness, I thought, in important places. My hair was no longer cut with a black fringe across my very pale forehead. It was long, and Mama allowed me to twist it up with pretty combs. My face was not wide, like Yasko Sato's (my best friend). It was, Mama said, looking at me one day out in the garden, fragile, delicate as a piece of her finest china.

I blushed. Later, I raced to the glass to see for myself. It was, could I believe it?, delicate—*pretty*! Not a blemish on my skin, though Yasko had unpleasant pimples which sometimes oozed yellowy pus. I thanked all the gods I had such clear skin, and hated myself for feeling superior to Yasko when I knew I could take no credit for it.

I began to notice that boys had begun to notice me. Hiro, who never talked to me except to ask why I didn't eat more rice, then I wouldn't be so skinny, stopped teasing. When we were near each other, in school, or walking home, his eyes roamed my body, especially where my breasts bulged out the front of my kimono.

"Wish I could keep from blushing," I raged to Yasko one day, after Hiro, handsome and straight, had looked me up and down.

"You are fortunate." Yasko's eyes, dots in her pudgy face, followed Hiro, now laughing with a group of friends beside a fish market. "It's attractive to blush. It makes you womanly."

"That's old-fashioned," I pouted. I liked everything that was new.

My pen pal sometimes sent me American magazines; I drooled over the fashions. I read all the Japanese movie magazines about America. Would Betty Grable blush? Or Judy Garland? No. It was too silly.

"It's just too silly," I said to Yasko, stamping my foot. "I must rid myself of a bad habit."

"How?" Yasko absentmindedly pushed at a great pimple on the left side of her face.

"Well—I don't know; I'll think about it."

We rambled home in the late afternoon spring air.

In December of that year Japan attacked America.

Attacked America!

Where had Maine gone? Were the rocks blown up, the house where Mona lived? Why had we attacked the place I dreamed of? Impatiently, not shy, I asked the teacher where the place called Pearl Harbor was. Was it in Maine?

"No, no. Not anywhere near Maine," he assured me. "Your pen pal is sure to be all right, Kyoko." He knew of our pen pals, of course, for it was he who began the program. "Our emperor is right to have done this, of course." His face was sterner than when we got lessons wrong.

I smiled and bowed. In my heart I was not sure the emperor was right.

I waited, waited, hoping to hear from Mona, but I never did. Did she blame *me* for Pearl Harbor? I wrote to her, but my letter was returned, with a censor's mark.

Meanwhile I began the next phase of my schooling. I qualified for high honors. How, I can't tell you, for my mind was on the war, on Hiro, who went to war. But not before telling me that he was going to be a real hero. For me. Not before telling me that I was like a peach blossom in spring and, though his family wanted him to marry someone else, he wanted to marry me when he came back.

It was beside a countryside shrine near the river that he told me these things. *So bold, so modern. How do you dare?* my mind murmured, my eyes on the brown, rocky earth.

He touched my hand. "I am leaving, Kyoko. That changes everything. There isn't time for the old customs. Will you think of me?"

I raised my eyes to his, felt I was going to faint, so intense was his gaze. "Yes, oh yes," I whispered.

Gently, his lips brushed my forehead. A crane rose from the nearby riverbank and shadowed us. *A good luck omen.* We watched its long legs stream out, watched until it was a dot on the horizon, and then nothing.

We parted, I to cry into my pillow that night, just like the heroines of old. Nothing really changes.

I cannot, do not want to, write passionately about Hiroshima, for the passion was spent long ago. My parents and sisters were vaporized; I was burned, as if I were a bundle of dry kindling.

The greatest passion I felt, then, was for death. I spat, raged at gods and goddesses who had taken my family, but let me live. The town I knew, as I knew the ways of my own body, no longer existed.

Simply, no longer existed. The years in hospitals are hazy to me; I didn't care sufficiently to try to remember. Shimmering pain, endless operations. Voices that clucked and whispered. Like sliding screens, all the years slid into one another, a series of empty rooms.

Hiro came back. And married the girl, perfectly spared, whom his family had wanted him to marry. I saw him across the road one day. It was his half-concealed shudder of horror that made me run to the small glass in the two-mat room where I was living. I hadn't looked in a mirror for years, hadn't cared.

But it wasn't my face, of course. This was a shriveled, diseased peach blossom, cankered, scarred, the lips fantastically twisted, the eyes like ash. Nothing to do with me.

Nothing to do with me. I ran screaming from my room towards a wood, hoping the foxes would find me, would devour me.

Instead, the authorities found me and put me with the other hibakusha.

What strange jobs I held through the years, when I *could* work. Of course, I never married. A shriveled bough is useless. And ugly.

One year a man came from America. He managed things so that some girls (had I ever been a girl?) could go to America for treatment.

To America!

I felt the flicker of my old dream. Surely they would

choose me. I stammered, babbled about my pen pal in the place called Maine. Surely my passion for America would burn through even my keloided face.

I wasn't chosen.

After my job sweeping out an office building was finished, I used to go to the sea. I would stand a long time staring across the dusklit water. Gulls summoned me.

"Come, come, it is so simple." They dipped, chattered, floated on the water like pure promises.

But I hadn't courage enough for an honorable suicide. I couldn't even do that. I felt the rough sand, rubbed my terrible face in its darkness, wailing for all I was. And was not.

A cousin, who had never come to see me, died and left me a bit of money. There was never any question in my mind what I would do with it. I would go to Maine. I would step into the postcard world I had dreamed of in the summer of my fifteenth year, when I had looked in the glass and had known that I was beautiful.

Of course there was a tangle of bureaucratic strings to get through.

But I am here! There is no Mona. It seems her family sold the house and moved away. Nobody knows anything about Mona. People here gulp, stare, and pointedly try *not* to stare at my loathed face.

I don't blame them, anymore. I know that silken geese sliding across the sky are more pleasurable to the eye than the crippled brown one, its damaged wing flapping dust.

A kind man rented me a small fishing hut near the very scene Mona sent me long ago. I explained, carefully, why I had come. As carefully, he listened. He is old, you see, and I am old. We speak beyond the face.

No one bothers me. The man has his own life and duties. I come each day to the splendid grey rock with this pad, to write, to draw. The sea thrashes beneath me. Some days there is one sailboat, some days many, some days none. The pines talk to me in an old language. Birds whir and speak, endlessly.

I *do*, after all, gather the immense white Maine daisies which blow wonderfully in the wind, their bright centers flashing light. I arrange them, not in a beautiful lacquered tray of my mother's, but in an old saucer found on the shack's shelf. I make a tokonoma. It is tranquil, absorbing.

I do not think of the time when I shall have to return, to be one of the hibakusha again. Perhaps I shall *not* have to return, for we all know that fate is unpredictable. Tomorrow the world may change utterly. It happened once in my lifetime. Who knows what the gods are planning?

I am happy. How many people can walk across the border into their dream and find it not lacking in any particular? Find it, in fact, enhanced by the sharp scent of wildflowers straggling beyond a postcard's lost dimensions?

The Minister's Wife

Mrs. Lamb adds a cake, her best church supper recipe, to the plethora of soups and casseroles littering the kitchen. Her face is properly serious, her conversation platitudinous optimism. She is earnestly good. And enormously boring. She tenterhooks over the word "death." For the Mrs. Lambs of the world people "pass on."

Miss Wilkins, a Sunday-school teacher for forty years, speaks in rustling tones of "losing" one's husband. I wonder whether I have misplaced Rob in the crush of the sales at Fuller's Department Store or on the last camping trip. I see him in limbo somewhere between "Bras—on sale" and the pines promenading down to the lake.

I knew Rob had been depressed. Daily, he found more excuses not to see old friends. The church meetings, once a challenge and delight, palled. He ducked them when he could. His preaching fell from inspired to pedestrian, and sometimes borrowed. When he appeared at the Installation of Officers service with dusty sneakers and a spotted tie, I knew the condition had slipped to serious.

Mrs. Lamb has put on the coffeepot and is going to make me eat. Why do people insist upon stuffing grief, as if one were a leaky boat? I shall never get through all the sacrificial offerings brought and will have to discard to decay these talismans. They *are* talismans: against loneliness, theirs and mine, against emptiness of spirit more than body; against death itself. If they cook and I eat we are still alive performing man's most basic ritual.

They bustle, the good grave ladies. And whisper. Why do they whisper? This autumn day is an anthem. Outside the kitchen window the maple is a fortissimo of color. Do they

49

believe Rob can hear them? So many meaningless rituals. It is an irritation to me for I hear isolated words only. They are speaking of Jason. Has he "been told?" Then, again, I cannot hear, and am irrationally furious.

"It is *our* death," I want to lash at them. "Jason's and mine. Why do you come into my home, my kitchen, and take it into your sanctimonious hands?"

Jason. Jason is at boarding school in Maine. He loves the wild of the woods, the sea running roughly away to far lands. At fifteen he is more man than boy, though his tight black curls, long, after a summer's freedom, are like a girl's. He hates the curls and spent hours of his boyhood trying to straighten them. He is very tall, and hates that, too. He writes poetry he shows to no one and attempts sports, which he also hates. Rob wanted him to be a minister, a demonstration of Rob's obtuseness. Wild, sensitive Jason, whose gods are woods and wild and waves and the solitary.

Poor Jason. Such a complexity of hates. More than I, in adolescence? More than most? I do not know. I shall phone him, unless one of the fussing ladies usurps the privilege. But not yet. I must not allow them to prod me into phoning too soon.

Another whisper. Something about wood from the pile in the garage. They want to make a log fire. Cheering. But dare they enter the garage? I will not aid them in their dilemma. They must face the specter there alone. Or *not* face it, as they choose. No one ventures the word "suicide," unless it is in one of the murmurs maddeningly low. They have not accepted it. Ministers of their God do not commit suicide, unless they are Episcopalians, a more sophisticated sect. I leave them to it. *I* would go to the garage but they would never allow it. They would cushion me like a piece of fine china packed for moving. But the car is still now. No motor idles, and I imagine all fumes of exhaust are dissipated. If Rob is "lost," it is not in that cramped space. It is far more likely that he is floating near the opaque saints in the stained glass window in the rear of the church, heroic and pious, in confettied light.

We stood together under that light, brightened by a blaze of Christmas candles. Not as bride and groom. I was an attendant at Susanna and Jake Wilbur's wedding. Rob was Jake's college friend and then minister. Our attraction was entirely overwhelming, but of course Rob wouldn't sleep with me. I was a nice girl and he had to marry me. Nice is a relative term, but I *did* marry him. The pasted-on smiles of my parents added nothing to the full-dress ceremony. They strongly objected, a provincial mistake I would not have thought them capable of. I was Italian and flammable, even as they. Our quarrels about Rob were rockets that never ceased firing. I had lived abroad, was "cosmopolitan," they said. He had grown up in a small town, was now a small town minister. I came of wealth and intellectualism. He was a grocer's son, they said.

They said and said, ad nauseam. I could not hear them, and ran, raving, to the phone to hear his steady, plodding voice, the Midwestern timbre a patchwork-quilted haven.

They didn't know I was pregnant. Rob did, but it didn't matter. After his first gulping shock, I think he felt I was a mission. Sent straight from God for him to save. I didn't marry him to "give my child a name." I would have had an abortion in a minute. Sam Hansberry was nothing but a summer wave, the quickening in my belly a kink in chiming water gone to other shores.

Rob wouldn't hear of an abortion. My mistake was in telling him at all, but there it was. He had gone to dinner and ordered wine (the only time I ever saw him drink anything). I had too much and maundered into sentimentality.

Sex was stronger than saving, at first. He was better at it than anyone I had known. And I had known some.

The church people made overtures. Jason was premature, of course. They told me of their own preemies and how well they had done. I blinked and listened.

But I wasn't prepared for the life. The meetings, the ever-open door, the phone at all hours, the meals for everyone, their need to know the fine points of our personal life, the suppers and circles.

51

Most of all, the awful, eager goodness.

I was entirely bored.

Summers gave me some respite. For the month of August we went to Maine. I wallowed in the wild freedom, away from the manse that never welcomed me. Not *really* welcomed me. I was too "different" and "a snob." Yes, even then they whispered. Maine absorbed me as I was. I was baptized new in those chill seas. Jason and I roamed beaches. We found shells and made castles, sometimes in the air. He scribbled verse I never asked to see. Rob fished, a bit, but mostly planned his winter: great sermons with metaphors of sea and sand and rock.

Sex slunk from marvelous and every day to sporadic and stolid. I have never hated anything as much as I began to hate the love of God. Rob took to preaching about fallen women. It was not my fancy that saw his manner to Jason, Sam Hansberry's child of summer, subtly shift.

Finally, they are going. It has taken all my tact and a good deal of posturing to avoid having them spend the night with me.

"You should not be alone," they clichéd.

"I adore being alone," I wish to shriek at them.

I want to think, alone, about Rob. I want carefully, with a martini in front of that log fire (it was Miss Wilkins, ramrod stiff, who finally bearded the garage), to think.

"Your nerves—you really should *not* be alone."

I manage to make them go, exhausted by the effort.

My nerves. They *were* bad. Mr. Rollins at the drugstore was very kind about renewing my prescription over and over again, though three times only is marked on the bottle. I collected closetsful of bottles.

I mix a martini. It nuzzles into me. The fire leaps shapes. I look around the living room, which has seen so many meetings, so many ardent church members. The couch is sagging and is a dreadful dun shade. The rugs are undistinctive, the lamps ordinary. I hate it. Like Jason, I am a complexity of hates. My parents could easily have made pleasanter the setting of our daily lives. They did nothing. I had made my bed. Detached, unfamilial, they watched me lie in it.

The room begins to float, mildly. The bleeding Jesus on the wall is appallingly sad. Did he ever laugh?

"Have a martini," I offer him. "Enjoy, enjoy." The brooding eyes stare on.

It is time to think about Italy. In two months all the rituals will have been accomplished here. I will be in need of a trip to recuperate, and Jason, like a good son, will accompany me. Of course we will not return. Rapello will speak to Jason, as will the mountains and the sea. Fig trees will hold him in their still shadows. He will sip Rome into his blood.

I thank Rob for his small cache of insurance.

In Italy I will teach English, I think.

One phone is in the bedroom. It is time to call Jason. He will be shocked but not undone. Rob was one of his hates.

I rise like a balloon to the bedroom, no strings dangling. There is a full harvest moon. And slithering over everything is the peace that passeth all understanding.

I will pack the empty pill bottles. All those pills I never took but gave so slowly, so carefully, away to Rob.

A wifely act, good, earnest, unselfish.

The Return

Something, I think, to do with the remembered warmth of the mother's womb. It *is* remembered; I am sure of that, in the subconscious that holds our verities, our necessary realities. A need to find again the place that once provided haven.

Haven. I looked it up one July morning on the piazza below my pensione in Rapello. It was the morning after Jason had come with his second wife, Maria, a girl half his age with astonishing hair the color of hay bronzed by the noon sun, and eyes the color of the swollen plums in our garden. She was plump as a ripe plum, too. Odd, for Jason had always been drawn to thin, taut women, like greyhounds poised at the starting line.

"She's a haven, Angelica." Jason had never called me Mama or Mother, to my former husband's keen annoyance. Rob felt it was significant, that it spoke of wantonness. He was right.

His eyes followed the girl, who had gone to repair her make-up (light, almost unnoticeable) after dinner in the swallow-light evening.

"A haven? An odd reason to marry," I said, remembering Jason's immense passions of the past.

"You think so? I find it—necessary." His slim dark height cast a long shadow in the candlelit dining room. He rose, gallant and godlike, as Maria returned.

And then they left, hand-in-hand like children, which she almost was and he, I felt, wanted to be again. Maria was surely some psychological need to recapture his youth, and perhaps other things I had no interest in facing.

But the word, haven, moved through my dreams that night like a streamer the color of fire. It moved from scene to scene like a message.

Which I needed to pay attention to, I decided over morning coffee and rolls. And so, as a beginning, I looked it up. It seemed in some vague but important way that I had never really understood it.

Haven: a harbor or port. Any place of shelter and safety; refuge, asylum.

Harbor. Suddenly I saw again the long road running down the hill in Maine to the beautiful harbor at the bottom, saw the rough wooden deck stretched out over the water, its benches where I had sat with my face full to the northern sun, warmed by it as my mother had never warmed me, except perhaps in the womb, where she had no choice in the matter.

I needed, needed terribly, to see it again, Maine. Needed its cool detached woods which yet were welcoming, just as I had needed them years before when I fled from the stifling small town where my husband, Rob, had been a minister and I had been his rebellious wife. I needed the slap of icy water against creaking pilings, the occasional glimpse of the wildness of a black bear.

Mostly, I needed the whack of it, the spanking of cold to rescue me from the cocoon of Italian somnambulancy. At sixty I needed more than La Dolce Vita, lyrical and hedonistic. Had something of Rob, imagine it!, filtered through my pores, something stern and puritan? Nonsense. Rob's unwavering stance, on everything, was what I had fled. Simply, I needed a change.

I really thought that was all, which shows how we can receive messages and misread their meanings.

Jason and Maria came to the airport to see me off at the end of July.

"You wasted no time, Angelica." Jason's eyes, full of questions, flicked into mine.

"No; I wrote the realty company, not any longer owned by Ike Roberts, somebody, now, named Lena Perkins. She had a small house I could rent for six months. Overpriced, of course, but—" I shrugged into the roar of jets.

"What are you going for?" It was Maria who, smiling, questioned me. "We don't want to lose you."

But I found no sense of loss in her. I was simply Jason's mother, an aging woman of sixty who should have been content, her eyes said, to stay in my small pensione with a son and new daughter-in-law. A shame, I thought. Too bad that security sat in her eyes like a cow in a pasture. Was *that* what Jason called haven?

"We lived there once, Jason probably told you. I had a dream. I wanted to see it again...."

"Yes." But she didn't understand. No more than Jason, though he would not press me further. Jason believed in privacy, as I did myself.

We waved, they from the clamor of Rome, I from the cabin of the bird I thought would fly me to some sort of haven. I sank back into the comfort of wilting flowers and books they had pressed on me. Some sort of haven. Or did I mean escape? Retreat?

"It's got warts, everything has, but it's fitted against the weather, handy to things and has its own kind of charm." Lena Perkins, a tall craggy woman of—fifty?—handed me the keys to Calm Cottage, a name I fervently hoped would find its reflection in my psyche. "Two storeys, as I wrote you, two bedrooms, one bath, a hankie of a yard you can work into something, if you're that kind, though yards are rocky, here. Nothing, I imagine, like Italy."

But I wasn't going to tell her anything of that other life, not now, anyway. Maybe not ever. Privacy was what I wanted.

"I'll enjoy getting it into shape," I said, looking at the tangle of weeds. "Good for the hands and head." I smiled.

"Yeh-up," her Maine twang surfaced. "Cold here in winter. You need to be good company with yourself." Questions hovered behind her words.

"Fortunately I am. Probably there's lots going on, anyway. Small villages are always remarkably busy places when the tourists go."

"You haven't an Italian accent," she ventured.

"No. I lived here and in New Jersey before I went abroad. Remember I wrote Ike Roberts, whom I knew well, and was turned over to you?"

"That's right, forgot."

But she hadn't; she was much too sharp for that. She wanted to know more, but I wouldn't bite.

"Call me if anything's not right. Lots of firewood there for later. All the furnishings are complete, far as I can see. Nothing you should need to get except your own frills." Which any lady who has lived in Italy will surely need, her spartan Maine figure implied. Or was I reading too much into simple friendship?

I laughed. "I'm sure everything will be fine, Miss Perkins. I appreciate all you've done to make the house comfortable. We'll see each other in the village. Thanks so much." I eased her towards the door.

"Yeh-up, we'll meet. Everybody knows everybody around here, after the hordes go home." She marched straight-backed down my pathway to her little car and drove off without a backward look. She *had* been friendly, Maine friendly.

I did need a change.

I only hoped I could give myself to it.

I turned back to the small living room, delighted to see that the fireplace was all the real estate broker's description said: large, with a white mantel over it, and above the mantel there was a built-in mirror. All was plain, hardy as the state itself. Someone had laid a fire in the grate, ready for lighting. Lovely. It might even be necessary to light it, for August nights in the north are chancy. And I'm the type who lights a fire for its ambience as well as warmth. It takes the chill off loneliness.

But I wasn't lonely. I've always loved being alone. What I had hated most about being a minister's wife was the endless numbers of people I had to accommodate, always keeping the essence of me from them, always having to be careful not to offend.

I let my suitcases sit on the woven early American rug and on an impulse walked round to the small garden in back.

Great yellow and orange marigolds moved in a gentle wind, like tiny suns. Zinnias, all hues, white and mauve petunias all struggled in straggly fashion, for life in the weedy maze. I was able to gather a small bundle of marigolds and zinnias, enjoying each single bloom I snipped with a tiny golden knife kept on my key ring, a gift from Rob long ago. I had thrown out almost everything that might remind me of him. Don't know why I kept the knife except that it was useful, often, for odd things.

Back in the house I arranged the flowers in an old blue-and-white jug found on a top shelf in the kitchen furnished with plain polished pine table and chairs. I brought the bouquet into the living room, set it on a table by the window which looked out on the street, beyond which was a field. There was no house directly across from mine, I was glad to see. The field was wild and beautiful in late-afternoon sun.

"I feel at home," I said to the flowers, to the room, to the house that was to be my own haven for a while.

I turned to pick up my cases, to take them up for unpacking.

And stopped, rooted. In the mirror, the reflection of the flowers dissolved to something like features: bottomless eyes, a nose, an open bright orange mouth. *A man's face.*

I whirled to the flowers. Innocently, brilliantly, they sat on the plain wooden table against the window now darkening at dusk. Slowly, I turned again to the mirror, breath held. But there were only the flowers crossed by shadows of late birds flying home. My breath whooshed out.

"Foolish woman," I said aloud to dispel the stillness. I flicked on the lamp beside the fireplace and knew I should have to light the fire that night to burn away such silliness.

My bedroom was papered in an old-fashioned design of cornflowers and ivy. The furniture, consisting of a single bed, dresser, wardrobe, and one straight chair, were of plain pine. The white spread on the bed was fresh, peaceful, inviting. Folded on the end of the bed was a handmade quilt of many colors.

I was suddenly exhausted. Jet-lag after the trip to Boston,

another from Boston to Bar Harbor, a bus down from Bar Harbor to Castine, finding Lena Perkins. The little white bed beckoned.

But so did my stomach. It had been a long time since food on the plane. I had no provisions yet. I looked out the small bedroom window. It wasn't quite dark. Perhaps I could find a small cafe open on the main street, or near the dock, which might still be crowded with tourists.

I went down the polished wooden stairs, locking my door, though Lena Perkins had said, "We don't lock doors here. No need to; you probably remember that." Yes. It was one of the most endearing things about the little town, and maybe I'd come to it again. But I wasn't quite ready, yet, for so trusting a stance. There were a lot of years between then and now, years and emotions.

The bright flowers were like a beacon in my window as I passed.

There were lights in some of the fine-looking white clapboard houses on my way. The library, facing on the wide commons, was solid, reassuring. Beside it the poet Robert Lowell's house was visible through structures of scaffolding. I made a left on the steep main street that ran down to the dock and the water, remembered with fondness from that other time. Two inns, one on the left, one on the right, were brightly lit. Warmth dappled the path before me.

"Perhaps I should have stayed at an inn," I mused to myself, and immediately thought better of it. No. I wanted my own space, no breakfasts or dinners with others unless I chose that companionship.

There used to be a restaurant to the left of the dock, I remembered. That would do well if it was still there. I came to the parking lot, still filled with cars. Very few people were on the dock. Tourists must be dining or drinking, or both, at various establishments around town. I walked out onto the dock, a small wooden square with a roof over part of it for shelter. How stable the old wooden planks, the pilings. A rush of affection overtook me. How I had loved this place, after Rob's death. It had indeed been a haven. Would it be again?

A sailboat bobbed at dockside, reached by steps on each side of the upper deck on which I stood. An Irish setter, its red coat painted almost black with shadows, slept on the boat's deck, oblivious to the gentle swell, the few staring people. To the left was the restaurant I remembered, its bright umbrellas on its large deck folded up for the night. Inside, lights cheerily burned, dotting the dark water. To the right the *State of Maine*, a training ship for the Maine Maritime Academy, loomed out of darkness, immense, reassuring.

What did I need reassurance for? *Jet-lag; I'd better get food and get to bed.*

I was led to a booth looking out on the harbor, ordered lobster, which I'd craved on the long flight over. First, though, a martini glistened before me. I lifted it, wanting, needing, its boost.

"*God!*" I stared at the glass quivering in my hand, spilling its contents on the plastic table top. *His face floated, green, hollow-eyed, in the pale liquid.*

"Is anything the matter? Are you ill?" The waitress moved to my side. "You called—"

"No." I put down the glass, my hand shaking. Had I called aloud? "No. Thanks." I swallowed. "Just forgot to take a pill I should have." I smiled, pretended to search through my handbag. "I'm fine."

"Another martini? Afraid you've lost most of that one."

"No, no. Just the lobster and—and the clam chowder, please." Though I wasn't sure, now, that I could eat.

"Of course. I'll bring the soup right away, and your salad." She deftly wiped up the spill before going to the kitchen.

I looked around at the room full of people laughing, drinking, eating. Everything normal. The dregs of my martini reflected only a ceiling fan idly rotating. I stared into the glass. But there was nothing, nothing but that slow, lazy revolution. I took the glass up in both hands, gulped down what was left of the searing liquid.

The evening of Rob's death came to me as though someone were running an old film in front of my eyes. The stillness after the chattering, over-kind church women had left, the martini I had relished afterward, toasting the blessed stillness, the sad portrait of Jesus on the wall, the thought of Maine as haven, and Jason.

"Chowder, nice and hot, do you good." The young waitress plopped a steaming bowl in front of me. "Find your pill?"

"Eh—oh, yes, yes thanks. I'm just fine now." I took a sip of soup, the plain wholesome fare like a poultice on my jangling nerves.

I really am dead tired. How absurd. That's all behind me.

I did, in fact, take an aspirin from my purse, and down it.

The bright, brisk conversations of other diners moved into me. *This is good solid rocky Maine, in summer abloom with tourists fleeing the clamor of cities.* No ghosts here. Isn't that why I chose it, after the disturbing dreams I'd been having in Italy, when I chased the word "haven?" Desperately. Though I hadn't told Jason of that terrifying desperation. How could I have explained it? I couldn't explain it to myself, safe and comfortable in the sun-easy landscape of Italy, miles and years away from Rob's church.

The lobster was fresh from the sea's cold water, wonderful, the salad tangy with a sort of gingery dressing, the baked potato basic and filling. Strong coffee and a liqueur entirely restored me, made me able to smile at fantasies of a long-dead husband, brought on, I felt sure, by that horror of travelers, jet-lag. After all, I had long ago come to terms with widowhood.

I paid my bill, walked up the hill, past the still-lighted merry inns, turned to my own little house with its lamp and nest of flowers welcoming me.

Haven. Yes, it was.

In half an hour I was asleep. The sleep was dreamless, deep, satisfying as the nearness of the sea I loved with its waves that, again and again, covered all beneath it, erasing all pasts.

The first order of business in the morning had to be provisions, then the renting of a car. I longed to visit remembered places: Mr. Desert Island, Portland, Casco Bay.

I breakfasted at a cafe on a side street and was able, through one of the inns, to rent a small car which, marvel of marvels, would be delivered to me at the inn in an hour. I sat on the airy porch of the inn, watched a group of bicyclers who'd spent the night there get ready to leave on their journey. Leggy, crisp, confident. Americans. One would know them anywhere in the world. *Like Rob.* No. Roughly, I pushed the thought away. These young people joked, laughed, wrapped in enjoyment, as Rob never had been. Joyless, judgmental Rob.

Speak no ill of the dead.

It was my long-gone Italian grandmother's voice that nicked me on this lovely August morning in Maine, U.S.A., lively with birdsong and the mewing of an orange cat who sidled near.

Abruptly I stood up as a small maroon car pulled up in front of the inn. After the necessary formalities I took possession and drove off, waving to the cyclers, to do my marketing.

Which, in two hours, I'd stored away in cupboards and the little refrigerator in my bright kitchen. I changed to old clothes, set off to wrestle with weeds that wanted to overcome the sparkling marigolds and zinnias. I'd bought a few basic tools on my shopping trip.

Immediately, I was absorbed. So fulfilling to deal with roots, the clearing out of old things so the new may grow. And prosper. And bright among the weeds were the flowers planted by someone who had enjoyed this house, this plot. I probed, dug, worked my way around rocks. Rocks! Oh! Towards the very back I'd build a rock garden, there in front of the remnants of a stone wall. Sedum of all types, primroses. I planned it in my mind, sun burrowing into me like an animal against winter.

The white bones lay at the bottom of a hole where I'd dug up a particularly arrogant clump of weeds. Pale, stark, mottled with droppings of earth shaken off the weeds' roots, they moved before my eyes. *Moved.* My head spun in the hot sun, as it had never spun in Italy's burning sunlight.

Rob's skull formed as I watched. I knew it, knew it, even minus the flesh and hair I had so intimately known.

I screamed, shrieked, unable to steady my head or hands. The face smiled up at me, obscenely benign, the sun, birds, trees tilting as I fell, face forward, over the hole.

"Steady, friend. Are you all right?" A strong hand touched me, turned me over among the rocks and stalks.

I blinked into the face of a youngish woman, about thirty, brown as bark, concern the only lines on her fine features.

"I—did I—?"

"You screamed. Guess you fainted. The sun *is* hot today." Her voice was relieved. "I'll help you get up; we'll get in out of the sun and I'll get you some water."

"It was the bones," I blurted, unable to stop the words.

"Bones?" She looked bewildered. "Um—you've a touch of arthritis, maybe?"

"No. Oh, no—in the hole." I was now sitting up, the hole uncovered before us.

She peered into it. "Yes. There are bones. Mrs. Rice's old retriever's, I imagine, or one of 'em. Two died on her. She planted 'em both in her garden. Oh, too bad if they disturbed you."

"Retriever?" I gulped. "Dog bones, you mean?"

"Yes, must be." She lifted out the horrid things. I shuddered. "What a shame—no way to greet a new neighbor." She slipped the bones, to my horror, into a voluminous smock with pockets. "I'll toss them out in my trash. I'm Amanda West. From the house next door." She indicated a small frame house to the left. She held out a hand. "Welcome. Come on to my house and I'll make you a cup of tea."

"But—" I took her hand, so strong, sure and clasping. "I saw—the bones looked like—" I couldn't finish.

"Not human, I assure you." She laughed. "Not a chance. All the Rices are buried in the churchyard of the Episcopal church, have been for centuries. No, her retrievers, I'll stake anything on that." She half pulled me to my feet as she spoke. She dusted me off and moved me with calm assurance towards her house, white and calm as a dove.

I was horribly embarrassed. "What a fool you must think

me. I traveled here yesterday from Italy, a long trip, terribly tiring. Must have done something to my nerves." I managed a tentative laugh.

"Oh, jet-lag can do it. Maine'll restore you in no time. We're down to earth here. No pun intended." She grinned at the pile of weeds and tousled earth.

She was down to earth, was Amanda West. I liked her more and more as we sat sipping tea in her sunwashed kitchen done in pinks and reds, cheerful as the anemones that sat on her white table.

"What a fun winter we'll have," she said pouring more tea out of her pot with an old-fashioned cozy covering it. She knew about tea, the proper way to make it. "You can tell me all about Italy. I've never been out of Maine in my life, would you believe it, poor provincial creature that I am." Her laugh spun out again. It was clear Amanda West wasted no time in worrying about provinciality.

"Lucky, maybe." I laughed, too, unable to believe I'd been so stupid. How could I possibly recognize anyone's skull, anyway! What nonsense. I took a sip of strong Earl Grey tea. It was flavored with bergamot; it was marvelous. "Maine's wonderful. A person would never need to leave."

"Just what I think, really," she confided. "I'm from a farm near Bangor, but my husband's in business here. I love Castine." Amanda loved most things, that was evident. What a happy, sane young woman. She put me to shame. "Doesn't mean I don't want to hear about Italy, all the same."

"Well, I may not be here for the winter, but will be for the fall, as far as I know."

"Good! We'll talk on long fall evenings when the leaves have turned and we begin to hug our fires."

Wonderful, wonderful. She's just what I need.

"You've been so kind," I said, finishing my tea and rising. "But now I really must get back to that tangle in the garden."

"Sure you're all right? It could wait."

"No; it's been waiting long enough, I can see that. And I'm fine. I'm not usually such a fool, Amanda." I wanted her to believe that.

"Of course you're not, anyone can see that. We all take funny turns sometimes. My, if you'd seen me screeching at a spider in the bathroom last week...." The strong laugh billowed out again like a kite borne on a brisk breeze. "Come back soon, and I'm coming to your house for tea someday, I warn you."

"You certainly are!" Though I loved privacy, I wanted Amanda to come. She wouldn't outstay her welcome. Too sensible. And busy. I'd noticed the quilting frame in the room off the kitchen, and, on the corner of the table, cards that announced "Amanda West, hand-made quilts," with her address and phone number.

She watched as I went through the little gate between our yards.

I knelt to my task, steady as a post. I buried in the offending hole all my silly fancies. Dog bones! I was able to laugh.

Days were long and lazy, though I was not indolent. One comes to that too quickly in Italy. I mean I was unpressured. If I wanted to walk clear to the wind-pushed sea at the other side of the peninsula, I did that, over the hill and down the sweep to the stretch of water that seemed never to be calm, as it often was in front of the dock near "my" side. Nothing to stop the wind, I supposed, in its long journey across the world.

One day I walked to a village store and bought watercolors and a painting pad. I'd never painted in my life, though I loved the galleries, the sculptures that brought culture-lovers, hungrily, to Italy. Simply, I urgently felt the need to try my hand at it. Anyway, why not? Sun flashed on the street that ran down to the parking lot at the bottom, danced on the deck overlooking the water, sparkled gulls and sailboats lilting in the harbor. It sheened, even, the grey, dour anchored *State of Maine.*

Where would I set up my canvas chair and paraphernalia? Everywhere, scenes offered themselves, despite tourists meandering up and down streets, into stores, over the dock and deck.

I parked my things on a bench, ordered a hot dog and

coffee from the small food stand. It was utter delight to sit beside my gear on the bench, eating in sun and warm free air with the tangy hot dog, the steaming coffee. Lovely, lovely, the white sails, the gentle swells on the water, the unhurried ambience that lulled.

Tomorrow, I resolved, I would ride to Portland to see the restoration there, but today.... Quickly I finished the last of my snack. Before gathering up my stuff I peered over the deck railing. Far below, for the tide was out, a white duck quacked sternly to six small yellow ducklings that trailed after her in the shallow water. She moved to the pilings, began to peck at something—algae?—that appeared to be delicious, while the small ducklings milled around her, bright as toy boats. Fascinating, the tiny shining fluffs, fascinating the mother's earnest peckings, fascinating the easy peace of it.

I spent a full half hour, just watching, interspersed with comments from tourists who found the little domestic scene equally fascinating, and occasional "hellos" from townspeople I'd now come to know. Miss Perkins, scooting about showing property, who stopped for a quick snack; the owner of one of the inns, come down for a break; a young man from the *Maine* who seemed homesick (damn; did I look so motherly?) and often came to speak to me when he saw me on the deck.

I was *not* homesick. This, after all, after all Italy, though my son and daughter-in-law were there, this felt like home. Perhaps I would *stay* the winter in the cozy little house with its fireplace that had an excellent draft, I'd discovered, and Amanda next door if I wanted company, plus Mefistofele, a great black Maine cat who'd come to live with me.

"Now they're going away under the restaurant deck. Better pickings there, I suppose," a tourist who'd been riveted observed.

"Yes," I smiled after the disappearing little family. I must go too, if I wasn't to waste the whole day, though who could call it waste, time spent in simple richness?

I gathered my gear, decided I'd walk all the way to the point, on part of which was an old battlefield. I could paint there without too many people peering at my amateurishness.

Excited, I set myself a good pace, despite the chair and painting equipment. I'd found a way to tether them together; it wasn't so bad.

Only a young couple were on the point, half hidden behind one of the small hills, wholly wrapped in each other. I moved near the edge, unpacked my chair, paints, and pad. I sat a few minutes getting my breath. What angle would be best for a beginning? Beginning indeed; I'd never painted anything before—a bedroom, with a roller.

What did artists do? Sketch first, apply color later, or simply begin to paint with no pencil sketch to guide them? I decided on the simplest of pencil guidelines first, before beginning on a handsome large sailboat anchored just off the point. It moved up and down in the swells, its jade-colored hull shining against blue-greenish water.

"Who's to see, anyway?" I made a first tentative stroke and felt like God Herself creating the world.

Nothing marred the perfect afternoon. In late afternoon I held the painting away from me. Adequate, I decided, not to be ashamed of, at least. And what fun it had been. When I went back to Italy I knew what I would do to banish indolence, boredom. *If,* I corrected myself. If I went back. But I needn't think of that now.

I walked back, slowly, easily, watching with a new eye the patterns dusk made on the road. I treated myself to a good dinner on the dock: a marvelous shrimp cocktail, lobster again, fluffy lemon meringue pie, a good bracing wine. Wonderful to have no one to answer to, no one to be responsible for. Wonderful, the delights of freedom.

Replete, at close to nine P.M., with satisfaction in my work and splendid food, I opened the door to my house, now left unlocked. Amanda's lights were on next door. I thought of running in to show her my work, but decided, after all, the walk had made me tired. I'd show her the painting tomorrow, with good sunlight on it. I grinned that I felt brave enough to show it to her. Mefistofele rubbed against my weary legs, meowed to let me know it was well past his suppertime.

"In a minute," I told him, glad of his welcome, his presence that demanded nothing more than a dish of cat food.

I dumped my gear in the hall closet but propped up the painting against a chair near the living room fireplace. I wanted to enjoy it! Why not?

After settling Mefe with a liver-chicken combination he loved, I ran a tub. The long dusty walk had tired my well-over-thirty muscles, however much I'd enjoyed it, and I was sweaty, painty. A quick wash in the waterfront restaurant's women's room hadn't addressed the extent of grime and grass stains.

I stripped myself of perspiration-soaked clothes, tossed them in a hamper, and poured lavender bath salts into the water. Mefe hopped up on the wide tub ledge, near the faucets, as I was about to step in. He cast a long black shadow on the water. His eyes gleamed, a greeny gold.

"Want to go out after your meal?"

But he seemed quite content to sit, watching, purring.

"Good puss." I patted him, stepped into his shadow, letting myself down into the warm, scented sea.

Mm. It's not often you know when you're happy. You only understand it in retrospect, usually. This night I knew that I was utterly, hedonistically, happy. It had been wonderful to work hard at something, wonderful to stretch muscles long unused. I felt as contented as Mefistofele grandly surveying my bath.

I closed my eyes. Gulls I had tried to paint soared across my inner vision.

"Ye-ow."

Mefistofele's back arched, suddenly, the hair on it standing up, his eyes become two slits.

"What's the matter, Mefe? Hear a mouse rattling in the floorboards?"

He gave a great leap and raced off towards the living room.

"I suppose *now* you want out, just as I'm relaxing. You'll have to wait a few minutes, Mefe."

I soaped myself with the Yardley's lavender soap I loved, carefully, lingeringly. I was out to pamper myself, the final touch on a beautiful day.

Done, I toweled myself, put on a white cotton nightgown (so cool, cotton in hot weather), and a light Chinese red bathrobe Jason had given me two Christmases before. Red slippers to match, a gift to myself.

"Mefe, Mefe," I called. "Time to go out." I made a whispering summons he usually responded to.

But he didn't come. Well, he'd come, rubbing and purring, after I settled myself in a chair. I'd only turned on one light in the living room when I came in, anxious to feed Mefe and get rid of dirt. So the living room was full of shadows. I switched on two more lights. A little too warm for a fire, though I didn't need much excuse to light one.

At last I sank down into a fine mauve velvet-covered armchair, an antique bought downtown, another gift to myself. I loved it. I positioned it so I could see my painting full on.

Time to assess my talent, or lack of it.

My God.

I arched up, a-bristle as Mefe had been, my shaking hand stuffed into my mouth which could only form screams.

Rob's face stared at me from the canvas.

Stern, as always unsmiling, it hovered in the faint outlines of a sail which billowed as if in a stiff breeze.

"Ye-ow!" Mefe scratched at my legs, tore at them, brought blood to the quivering surface of them.

"No, no." I kicked Mefe away, spun to my bedroom, fished in my handbag for my keyring, for the gold-handled knife.

"Damn you, damn you, leave me alone." Back in the living room I lashed at the painting, screaming, thrusting at Mefe who leaped at me, possessed.

I raced for the front door, flung it open and ran, in my night things, screaming down the path until I stumbled, and all was blackness.

"Here she is, opening her eyes." Amanda West smiled at me, her uncomplicated face a room that offered endless comfort.

70

I opened them even wider. White walls, dangling equipment. "I'm—I'm in—the hospital?" I was amazed. "What am I doing here, Amanda?"

"Cat scratched you pretty badly, love, and you fainted on the walk."

I was jolted into remembrance.

"God, oh God, it was Rob—Rob there in the painting, Rob, he won't leave me alone. God, my God, I murdered him."

Amanda moved swiftly to me. "Angelica," she took my two hands in hers, "Steady, you've had a shock. The cat...."

"It wasn't the cat," I shrieked. "Didn't you see—in the painting? Rob, my husband. That I murdered. God, God." I wrestled my hands from hers, tried to get out of bed, but her firm strong hands held me down.

"Angelica, the painting in your living room was only of a sailboat—off the point, I think. What painting do you mean?"

I stared at her. Did she think she could fool me?

"You know it's Rob. Mefe knew, didn't he? My murdered husband," I whispered, shaking, shaking.

"We went into the living room, after bringing you here, to make sure everything was all right. The only painting there was the one of a sailboat you'd slashed. It was pretty good, Angelica, what I could see of it. You didn't have to ruin it." Her voice moved smoothly. Soothingly, she thought, I guess.

"I was knifing *Rob*. I tell you, he won't stay dead, damn him."

Amanda bent over me, ran her hand over my burning cheek. "We heard from Mary Carter, in town, who lived here when you first came here, long ago, with Jason, about Rob, Angelica. About his suicide; that was a terrible thing to have to live through, my dear. Something here must have brought it all back to you. Maybe you shouldn't have come back to Maine, Angelica."

"Suicide? No. Oh, no. Don't you understand? I murdered him. You've got to believe me. Otherwise," I sobbed as into a long dank passageway, "I'll see him forever, in everything."

"We'll phone Jason, Angelica. He'll come and take you

71

home to Italy. You can forget Maine and its unpleasant associations, maybe see a doctor who'll help you. I'm just a country girl, dear, but I know you need a doctor, one who'll help your mind. A few months in the sun in Italy, you'll be fine." Amanda spoke as if she were covering me with one of her handmade quilts.

"No, not Jason, not Italy," I cried. "Don't you see it doesn't matter where I go unless you believe me?"

But she was busy summoning a nurse who came in, bright with benevolence, and a needle she thought could cure me.

"No, no," I sobbed. "Listen...."

"Won't hurt, dear. It'll give you some rest and when you wake up you'll see it all differently." Briskly, she jabbed me.

"Terrible," I heard her whisper to Amanda as I slipped into the bottomless black sea, "what suicides do to survivors. Poor woman."

Last thing I heard was somebody chuckling.

Hanging in There

I used to spend most Sunday mornings hanging Billy Walker in the last pew of the Congregational church on Greene Street in Philadelphia. One Sunday every two months I had to sing in the kids' choir, but the rest of the time we played hangman in hymnbooks. Somebody, old Johnson the sexton, I guess, changed the books, or laboriously erased and never told. Anyhow, we hardly ever got the same books and so had pure white pages to decorate. Sometimes we got tired of hangman and just drew pictures, strange spaceships inhabited by stranger creatures.

Billy's middle-aged father (we thought him ancient) snoozed beside us through the sermon. We drew only through the sermon because we liked to sing hymns full voice. So did Mr. Walker—fuller. He sang like a train going through a tunnel at full speed. I mean it wasn't only loud, but two bars ahead of everyone else. He always stopped with a mildly surprised air. You could tell he wondered why everyone else was dragging their tonsils. But he never seemed to figure it out, for the performance was repeated in the next hymn, Sunday after Sunday. For a tin can tycoon Mr. Walker was pretty dumb.

All the real action took place in the choir loft when the adult choir sang. I discovered that the Easter Mary Ellen Jones and I got Bibles given to us for perfect memory work. Mary Ellen was one of those girls born with white gloves on and manners, so you can see she had no trouble. My father was the minister or I'd never have made it. But when you have God sitting over you at breakfast, lunch, dinner, and the cracks in between, you think three times at least before you skip memory practice for baseball.

Anyhow, that day we got to sit with the choir, which was right behind the pulpit. There was a little door in the short wooden partition separating choir from pulpit. Luckily. If it hadn't been there my father would have had one made. (He'd never have made it himself; he couldn't tell a pair of pliers from a hammer.) Throughout the whole service he used that door. I'll tell you about that in a minute.

It all began with the caged white mouse parked just inside the door on the choir side. My white mouse, Samantha. I don't know if she was a girl. She hadn't had any children, but it was the name of the girl who sat in front of me in school. She had the whitest teeth you ever saw and a nose that wiggled. You notice things like that.

Father was a great one for graphic sermons. Like the Sunday he brought in one (sliced) loaf of bread and five lank fish. Whether he was able to make the whole congregation believe that little offering could have fed multitudes I don't know. Knowing my father, he probably managed it. I was too busy hanging Billy to listen, but I remember pungently the odd odor that permeated all the way to the back pew by the end of the service.

Samantha was supposed to illustrate something about being trapped. "Rat in a trap," you know, though I don't know how Samantha felt about being called a rat. It may have been what set her off, for Father managed to work the phrase into the Invocation.

From the beginning the ladies in the choir front row eyed Samantha with suspicion.

"Isn't she cute," Florence Byers frowned.

"As long as she stays in the cage," stout Nancy Allen laughed. Nervously.

Samantha, in my old hamster cage, couldn't seem to settle down, and I couldn't blame her. The pulpit was packed with flowers and the whole place stank like a funeral parlor. It was busy, too.

Did I tell you that Father was the choir director as well as the minister? Also the tenor soloist? (There are some privileges—penalties?—to having a financially squeezed church.)

These things are what made the little door essential, you see. Father would come through to lead the anthem. Usually there was a solo as well, and if it was a tenor solo, and oddly it often was, Father came through to sing.

On Easter Sunday he really pulled out all stops. He threw in, all for the same price, a violin solo. By himself, of course. Mother was the organist, so you can see they had a corner on the music market. Energetic (however saintly) wall-to-saintly-wall music was what we had on Easter, a lot of it by Father.

Anyway, Samantha got on the wheel in the cage and raced round as if it were the Kentucky Derby. I felt sorry for her and thought about taking her out and holding her a while, but I didn't think Mary Ellen, sitting next to me prim as a pope, would appreciate that. Besides, I hadn't got my Bible yet and I didn't want to prejudice God.

I got up with everyone else to sing the first hymn. I *loved* to sing. I was my father's son. About midway through the first phrase I became conscious of an odd little stuck bagpipe beside me. Mary Ellen was a drone, a perfect monotone, in a register that must have appealed to dogs. It did not appeal to Samantha, I could tell, for her feet flew faster and faster. If she kept that up she'd have a heart attack and all the flowers would be able to serve some purpose.

I almost had a heart attack listening to Mary Ellen. In our family everybody could sing on pitch and read music. If you couldn't they sent you back for a new model. I pondered on how Father was going to react to having a permanent drone right through the service. He'd hear for sure; he'd never miss a thing like that. Father turned round once or twice, and, after locating the stuck stop, delivered penetrating darts with his eyes. Obviously Mary Ellen didn't know Father very well, for she kept right on. I had to admire her for that.

Samantha kept right on, too. Right through the anthem Father came back to lead with his usual large swooping motions, as if he had the Mormon Tabernacle Choir at his command. Fortunately, the choir at full voice drowned out poor Samantha's endless pattering.

We were next, Mary Ellen and I. We stumbled, at least I

stumbled—Mary Ellen pranced purposefully—through the swinging door for the presentation. I managed to smile at the appropriate place and even remembered to bark "Thank you" when Father gave me a black Bible with gold-edged pages and shook my hand. It was only by keeping my eyes on a distant fixed point, Mr. Walker's ample belly, that I managed the thing with any finesse. Mary Ellen, of course, did it all with the air of a grande dame only accepting her due.

We ploughed back through the maze of flowers, followed by Father, who came to get Samantha for his sermon. The poor little thing backed into a corner of her cage and began a queer moaning noise, soft but decisive. *Imagine! Mice can moan!* I marveled in my head. Firmly, Father picked up the cage, stalked back through the swinging door, and began. Through his gritted teeth I thought I heard him mutter something about Mohammed and mountains.

Surely Samantha would stop. Nobody moaned when Father preached. I underestimated Samantha. She moaned, continuously, just like Mary Ellen and her drone. The thing must be catching. I was so caught up in Samantha's problems (she squeaked at the top of her tonsils when Father rashly took her out and held her up to the congregation for a moment) that I missed the point of his sermon. Riveted, I watched Father thrust Samantha back into her cage, and just in time. I'd have bet on her biting him, or, shall I say it delicately?, worse, any minute. Father finished the sermon and brought Samantha back, depositing her with a withering look. Nobody upstaged Father, particularly not a white mouse.

He played a violin obbligato to the next hymn. So did Samantha, minus a violin. At least I don't think it was Father who squeaked up a tornado. At the finish of the hymn Father looked quite ready to take Samantha out and crucify her. Only thing that saved her was that it wasn't Good Friday!

I prayed, I really did, that Father would skip his tenor solo during the offering. It was like praying that Niagara Falls would run backwards. Father sang. Samantha squeaked and

raced. Florence Byers and Nancy Allen began to stuff hand-
kerchiefs in their mouths. Somebody in the bass section, I was
afraid to look to see who, had to leave in a fit of coughing.

In the middle of Father's solo!

He finished, red-faced and scowling. He raced through
the door to receive the offering, which was blessed in a singularly curt fashion. We staggered through a final hymn and Father came back to lead the "Hallelujah Chorus."

The front-row sopranos had recovered, though the bass
had the sense not to return for the final curtain. Things
started off rousingly, with the whole congregation standing.
The choir soared to the place near the end where everything
screeches to a halt before the final hallelujah. This is usually
what is known as a pregnant silence, if all goes well. It is every
singer's nightmare that one time, just one time, he or she
isn't going to count right and will belt out a "hallelujah" in
that exotic silence.

Well, no singer did.

Instead, Nancy Allen screamed at the top of her con-
siderable voice and fainted, graceful as a blimp, to the
red-carpeted floor. Trained by my father, the choir finished
the last "hallelujah," which shows you where my father stood
in relation to God, before a bevy of sopranos bent over
Nancy.

Father thundered out a truncated benediction. Easter
Sunday service was over for another year.

It was like a sixteen-alarm fire around Nancy Allen. And
Mary Ellen Jones, that girl who couldn't sing any note but
one during the whole service, was standing on a chair hitting
every key there was and a few extras. Out of the corner of my
eye I saw Billy Walker sprawled on the last pew in tears of
laughter.

I made for Samantha's cage. The door was open wide and
it was still and desolate as an empty tomb.

I never saw Samantha again. Or Nancy Allen either.
Would you believe a thing like a white mouse could make
anyone leave town?

Our choir didn't sing the "Hallelujah Chorus" for some

years after that. Father cut back on graphics and realism. I stayed in the last pew with Billy Walker just as long as I could. Hanging was a lot safer than that choir loft.

Samantha was the only tactical error Father ever made.

Praise, Rubens,
and Mrs. Greenwood

Every Sunday after service when the reverend stood at the door to greet people I'd wait my turn and then say to him, "You done fine, Reverend." I'd beam at him, shakin' his hand like mine was a dog waggin' its tail. He'd smile back, a sort of little boy grin, and say, "Thank you, Mrs. Greenwood. You don't know how much your good wishes mean to me." He'd vary the words a little, but not much. I could count on 'em, like the sun comin' up every morning.

But he meant 'em. I felt that, though his eyes were like water beetles in a pond, dartin' this way, that, who was in front of me, who comin' after. He meant 'em, because what man, thunderin' about God for a good twenty minutes or more (his wife sat in the front pew, watch in hand front and center, but he never looked at her) before a sanctuary full of people, don't want to hear they ain't bored them cross-eyed? Sometimes he *did* bore *me* cross-eyed, though I'm a great believer, but I figgered that was because of my lack a learnin'. If you was nose-tilted-towards-heaven Mrs. John F. Houston, III, who'd been, she dropped often into conversation like bricks from the top of a building, to college, you'd a understood, I guess, some of them words that floated over my head like balloons at the Sunday-school picnic held every June down by the creek. Colored, dancing in wind, completely uncatchable.

Anyways, as I say, who don't need praise in this life and maybe beyond? Even if you *get* to heaven I ain't so sure God'll have time to hand out compliments. I mean, think of the tons and tons of people linin' up, for instance, just for the Heavenly Bathrooms, though I blush to think of it. Maybe in heaven that's one of the things we're spared, needin' to move bladders and bowels like some sort of perpetual garbage disposal machines. If God has *any* sense He'll have us set minds and bodies on Higher Things.

Oh, I say we better do our praisin' *here*, given the odds against it *there*.

So I'd say, "You done fine, Reverend." Then, if it was Communion Sunday, which came around once a month, sure as a merry-go-round horse, I'd go back to the kitchen, where me and my friend Mrs. Elsie Smith washed up those skimpy little communion glasses. Y'know, you wouldn't offer a rattle-snake such scant hospitality, and no one'll ever convince *me* God means such a bare cupboard for them that comes to His supper. Likely it began with some bobbie-pin-lipped wife who first trickled out wine like it was medicine.

In the prayer-meeting/Sunday school room there's a big paintin' of Jesus and His friends eatin' the Last Supper. Can't tell me they had little dollops a wine like we get, those great big men, Peter fresh off a fishin' boat n'all. Why, it'd be like servin' Mr. Greenwood, bless the man, a thimble a beer after a day at the construction site. Over there in the desert (think of the dust that donkey must of kicked up on Palm Sunday), you *know* wine must a flowed like water never did. I remember that missionary we had two years back said the water wasn't fit to drink, full of bugs that ate your innards. So somebody got their signals crossed for sure, here. Not that we'd want a Saturday night party every Communion Sunday mornin', but wouldn't it be cozier?

We sit like statues in the park while the organ plays them hymns that come out like the music piped into funeral parlors. Wouldn't it be jollier if we all had our skins broke down with a really nice tumbler a wine? Soon everyone would be smilin', maybe cryin' out their real insides, and what, for God's sake, is wrong with that? We could just open our arms and comfort 'em. Someone might even laugh out loud. Don't tell *me* nobody told jokes at that Last Supper. Them rough men? Listen, I bet some blue ones passed with the purple wine.

"Helen, you're terrible," Elsie giggles. We've been drinkin' down the dregs of the communion wine. Well, you can't put bottles with only an inch or two in the bottom away till next time. There's no sense at all to that, and it's a little bonus, I tell Elsie, for us doin' all the washin' up. You don't see Mrs. John F. Houston, III, diggin' her hands into detergent.

"Plain sensible," I say, lookin' at a bottle a little fuller than the others. Worth savin'? No. Got to leave room in the cupboard for new bottles. Wasn't there somethin' about old vessels and new wine in the Bible? I can't think of it at this minute, but if I *could*, I know it would apply to this very situation.

"How's your diet comin' along?" Elsie has hung up the dishcloth after dryin' all them little mean glasses. Hands on her hips, she eyes me, up, down, around. "Lost a bit, ain't you?"

Now it is time in this story to confess to you that I weigh two hundred and fifty pounds and am five feet two inches tall in my nude, you must excuse the expression, feet. Since Mr. Greenwood died, bless the man, eatin's been a comfort, though I must say it was a comfort before, too. I can't remember a time, truth to tell, when food *ain't* been a real solace. When Mama died leavin' me with two younger ones to raise (for Pa wasn't much of a hand at it, likin' his wine a bit too much), when, finally, he run off with that cashier down at the diner, (though what she saw in Pa is more than I could figger), after that, as I say, I just cooked up the biggest mess of pasta you ever saw. Ate the whole thing before the kids came home from school. It filled one leg, maybe. Didn't seem to reach my heart.

It was Elsie, one day at her house talkin' about my heart and things like blood pressure, scarin' me half to death, who fished out of a drawer full a strings and elastic bands a paper clippin' about some grapefruit juice and salad diet. "Safe," the article said, "and sure."

"You ought try it, Helen, you don't want to end up in Linville General Hospital on a breathin' machine. Try it.

Ain't no harm in tryin'.'"

Well, Elsie's been a good friend to me. We've played bingo together at the firehouse for years. When my one kid, Jeff, was killed by a hit-and-run driver they never found, and I went hollow as a cave inside, even after the five stuffed hoagies I ate, it was Elsie held me, well as you can hold two hundred and fifty pounds, and let her ironed cotton dress get soaked with my sobbin'. When Mr. Greenwood, bless the man, flopped dead, just like a fish out of water, at the site, it was Elsie came. Just like those Everlasting Arms in the hymn, Elsie has.

But, "Grapefruit juice?" I scowled. "Why, I'll be mean-lipped all the time, I drink that stuff." One thing I am not is mean-lipped. I smile a lot. People tell me I'm jolly. Good-natured. Easy goin'. You know. I'm a fat woman.

"There's a kind, the article says, that don't taste sour. Try it for just two days, Helen. What can you lose?"

"Couple a pounds, I hope," I laughed. "All right, Elsie, for you. Though you know I'm happy just the way I am; I'm just fine."

"Course you are," Elsie says, hand on my shoulder. "It ain't the way you *look* I'm talkin about; it's your health. Heart attacks ain't no fun, Helen."

I didn't say I'd had plenty of 'em. Attacks to my heart. What use to say things like that? People got enough troubles of their own.

"Okay, Elsie, for you, but I ain't makin' no promises."

Elsie shone like a sun come from behind clouds.

When she asks me today, us finished with communion washin' up, about that mouth-changin' diet, I feel guilty, like I never do feel in church, even.

"Couldn't do it more than a day, Elsie. God almighty, at the end of one day I was ready to eat the roaches that sit in my kitchen like kings. God never meant anyone to starve themselves, Elsie, I never seen that in the Bible."

Elsie sighs, right from her good patent-leather shoes to the top of her dyed red hair. "Oh, Helen, I don't want you to get sick. What would I do without you, anything happen to you?"

I see what she means. Elsie's husband is NOT THERE. Couple a strokes, a few years back, left him with the use of only one arm and leg, and a brain that thinks he's five years old. I make life worthwhile for Elsie, and I don't mind tellin' you the truth: she makes it worthwhile for me. We're lucky, Elsie and me, we got each other. Some people got nobody.

I put my arms around her. "Nothin' gonna happen to me, Elsie. I just *know*. Some people got vision. I *know* about my health. I'm one of those, what you call 'em, survivors. I *like* livin', Elsie. Ain't gonna let anything take life away from me. I'm on good terms with God, too. Who else is gonna wash His communion glasses," I laugh, "Mrs. High-and-Mighty Houston?"

Who came, at that moment, into the church kitchen, her arms full of red roses and feathery ferns.

"Elsie, Helen." She always calls us by our first names, though we call her Mrs. Houston; one of those things. "You've cleaned up all the communion glasses, how lovely." As though she don't know we always do it. Her eyes dart like disturbed bees to the empty bottles we ain't yet thrown away. "Just came to wrap these in damp towels for sick members. So nice to get flowers when one is ill. I'll take a bunch to Mrs. Lamb at the home, such a sweet old woman."

The home is a gorgeous place up on the hill the other side of town. I know I'll never get there; one of those things.

"On Tuesday we go to London for two weeks. Isn't that marvelous? Mr. Houston has business there." She is busy ripping paper towels from the wall holder, running them briefly under the faucet.

"London, England?" Elsie asks, eyes wide as the open roses.

"Of course." Mrs. Houston's laugh ripples silvery and brittle. "Tell you what, I'll send you both postcards." Her eyes linger for a moment on the empty bottles. It's clear she'd like to say somethin' but she ain't clear in her mind *what*. Frowning slightly, she takes up her bouquet and sweeps out, a whiff of musky perfume hanging in the dank kitchen.

"She won't," Elsie says, tossing bottles into the recycling bucket. "She won't never think of *us*, once she hits London, England."

"You can count on *that*." I help with the bottles. Actually, I feel moderately friendly towards Mrs. Houston. That's what communion wine does to you.

Elsie and I leave that kitchen clean as a licked plate, call to Bill the janitor that we're going, and go, she to cook Sunday dinner for her child-man, I to eat the big Sunday dinner I treat myself to every Sunday at the Ristorante Georgiano on Price Street. Such pasta! And red wine that don't cost the salary I make workin' part time at the K-Mart. Maybe I'll get my reward in heaven, like Reverend preaches all the time, but I ain't takin' no chances. I give myself one, here, every Sunday. God can deduct it if that's how He works. But I don't think He will. I think He's okay, like the reverend, doin' as fine as He can with what He's got to work with.

Three weeks later, first week in July, the rose season gone and Sunday altar flowers changed to zinnias and marigolds, I come home from work played out. Out of habit, not hope, I stick my hand in the mailbox in the hall downstairs in my roominghouse. Junk mail, like usual, and bills for sure. I clench the bunch and fight my way, step by step, like I'm climbin' a mountain, to the second floor. Only three floors in this place. No elevator, of course.

"Those steps," I'd said to Elsie yesterday at prayer meeting, "oughta make me thin, but they don't. That's why I don't exercise. It don't work." I believe it. Absolutely.

"Give you a heart attack, more like." Elsie had looked worried.

"We're gonna have a birthday party Tuesday," Elsie's husband had chimed in on the point of us sayin' goodnight after prayer meeting. "Balloons, Elsie says, games...."

"That's swell, Jim," I'd said. "You have a great time. Got a haircut, I see. Ain't you the handsome one."

Jim left, beaming like I'd already given him a birthday

cake, Elsie smilin', too, worry over my heart wiped away. "He's pleased as anything you noticed," she whispered.

Praise. Every time, it works.

Well, as I was sayin', mail in my hands, I drop into my large armchair by the door before even gettin' a cold drink from the fridge. I begin to sort through the bunch, lazy like, not carin' much, though I do like the flower circulars that sometimes come. Pleasant, coolin'. Mr. Greenwood, bless the man, and I had a small garden when we was first married. I thought there wasn't nothin' nicer than diggin' the cool earth, seein' worms wrigglin' away to maybe China, puttin' in those bitty seeds and, in a while, havin' color splash up, scented, too. Now *there's* a miracle for you.

When I see the postcard I sit up straight as the pole Mama used to prop up her clothesline with. From, would you believe it, London, England, from Mrs. John F. Houston, III. First I almost didn't know who it was from 'cause it was signed "Alexandra Houston," and I couldn't, you can understand, for a full minute determine who *that* was. But, like Reverend says, light comes.

"She didn't forget! Imagine. Wonder if Elsie got one, too. From London, England."

I turn it over. I want to tell you I almost have that heart attack Elsie keeps talkin' about, right then and there at 15 Gardner St. Apt. 2-C, Linville, in July of this year of Our Lord.

It is *nudes.* Large nudes, pearly white as the gardenias someone brought to Circle one afternoon. And two *men* gazin' at them, moony-like.

I swallow hard. Gulp is more like it. What is that woman doin' sendin' me a postcard of fat women? And them *nude*?

Fat women. My breath feels like someone is chokin' it off. No. Even Mrs. Houston couldn't be that mean. No. I am takin' it the wrong way, for sure.

I look at the printing at the top of the address side. "The Judgement of Paris, 1635–37, Rubens, The National Gallery, London," it says.

Paris? But Mrs. Houston was in London. Far as I remember, Paris is in France. It is as if someone has sprayed a fog over my mind. I shake my head, but it won't come clear. Who is being judged? Me? Is it something out of the Bible I never heard of? But there wasn't no Paris in Bible land, least *I* never heard no preacher speak of it. I pull at my left ear, as if it was a lever on a camera and everything will leap into focus. Nothing does.

Then I notice there is writin', too, beside my name and address.

We went through this marvelous gallery yesterday. It will warm you. I thought you'd enjoy knowing that in Rubens' time it was stylish to be plump.

P.S. I said nothing to Reverend Andrews about the communion wine.

Regards,
Alexandra Houston

Rubens' time? I stare at the small rectangle. Who is, was, Rubens? "1635–37," I read aloud. "That's over three hundred years ago." So it was "stylish" to be "plump" then. *But not now.* Is that what Madame Witch is sayin'? Does she think I wash feelins off nightly, same as sweat? And that about the wine. As if reverend would care. He's a regular person. That's why I tell him, every Sunday, that he done fine, even if I've gone to sleep the first two minutes.

"Witch." The word spins round the room, bumping into tables, chairs, knockin' over lamps, rufflin' up the carpet, bangin' on the window panes, my anger like a trapped bee.

I ease myself up from the chair, postcard still in my hand like it's cemented there, and go to the fridge. I get out the bottle of red Chianti I specially like, pour myself a full tumblerful. I plop a couple ice cubes in before movin' back to my chair. Carefully, I set the wine on the small table beside the chair and let myself down into it again. I take up the wine, take a good swallow, and hold the card in front of me, picture side to me.

I stare at the three "plump" women, the one with her breasts, for God's sake, full towards me, the bottoms of the other two like—like great white dahlias, I decide, that sometimes are brought in for the altar. As I stare and stare they become like *real* flesh, alive on the piece of cardboard.

I gulp more wine. What is the cloth half covering one? Velvet, maybe? And a—a peacock near her feet? Lord, there was a peacock at the farm next to ours, growin' up. I could of wrung the creature's neck, it shrieked so, ungrateful for its blessings of beauty.

This bird doesn't look like that. No green or blue, like the Johnsons' next door. It seems to move as I watch, twists its neck to look at me. Then the dog begins to stir. It *does*. Gets up and shakes its whole self. The lambs (just like the Johnsons') bleat weakly.

God almighty! I take more wine to steady myself.

Isn't that young Jeff in the left-hand corner, my Jeff who'd been dead for years? I begin to cry, and the child flies on its small wings to my lap. I rock him, rock him, tears like the Bible flood flowing everywhere.

It's a long time before I can get the child to sleep. I doze with him. It's dark when I open my eyes the next time. I can't see the card anymore. It has fallen to the floor. I grope for the lamp beside my chair, and switch it on. I lean down for the postcard. "Judgement, judgement." I can't understand it at all. I labor up from the chair, prop the card on the fake mantel over a fake fireplace. I pick up the phone and punch out Elsie's number. Five rings. Where is she?

"Yes?" Elsie's voice at last. She never answers with "Hello." I never ask her why. Elsie's entitled to her own self.

"Elsie," I pant. "Did you get a card?"

"A card? What d'you mean, Helen? It ain't bingo night. You been havin' Chianti?"

"A postcard, Elsie. From Mrs. Houston. Remember, she said she'd send us cards?"

"Oh. Sure, but I knew she wouldn't. What made you think of that?"

"Elsie, I *got* one. Today in the mailbox when I came home. With the bills and the junk circulars, a card from London, England, signed, believe it, 'Alexandra Houston.'"

"You didn't, you're kiddin' me, Helen Greenwood."

"It's right here on the mantel. The picture part says," I squint, "'The Judgement of Paris.' Queerest card you ever seen. Three hundred and fifty years old."

"Helen. You *have* been in the Chianti. Ain't no cards outside of museums three hundred and fifty years old."

"That's it. This is from a museum. In London. Painted, I guess, by somebody called Rubens. You ever hear of him, Elsie?"

"Only Ruebens I know is a sandwich. What's the card say, Helen? Read it to me, quick."

But suddenly I am shy. Somehow I don't want to read it to Elsie. Don't want to share my fat self. Not even with Elsie. See, it's just against my way of thinkin' to pass on mean things, even though maybe she didn't *mean* it mean, and I just took it the wrong way. Call me simple if you want. Maybe cowardly, I don't know. All I know is I ain't never seen no use to it, passin' on such things.

"I—can't, Elsie. Writin's hard to make out. Come over tomorrow; I'll show you."

Lettin' somebody read somethin' for themselves is different than announcin' it, like a bulletin, over the phone.

"But I can't, Helen. Jim's bent on goin' South to see his sister. She sent us bus tickets. He thinks it's a birthday gift. We're leavin' seven ayem for Georgia. I can't disappoint him, Helen. Doctor says he's in a real bad way, I better take him if he's to see his sister again." Elsie begins to cry, softly, like a bird in distress, if a bird could cry. "I was gonna call you later tonight," she manages when she can clear her voice.

"Oh, Elsie—" What can I say. I'm sorry Jim's so bad. Yet— what a burden he is to her. Life sure is always a plate with two sides. "Elsie dear, you and Jim have a fine trip. The card'll be here when you get back." Though I'm not sure it will be. "We'll laugh about it together." Though I don't see one thing in it that's funny. It gives me shivers, now, lookin' at it: a strange woman nude in a tree, a kind of a witch in a mirror. *What'd she send it for, anyway?* I swallow and say, "Anything I can do for you, Elsie?"

"Nothin' to do. Thanks, Helen. Helen, maybe my card'll come while I'm away."

"Sure, that's it. It'll probably be in your box tomorrow, after you've left." But I had a strange feeling that Elsie, ordinary-sized, a nice 12, unnoticeable to most folk, except for her brilliant red hair, wouldn't get a card from Alexandra Houston. What message was there for plain Elsie? Only I, all blubber and bloat, was *seen*. I mentally slap myself outa *that* mood.

"Bye, Elsie, give Jim a hug. I'll miss you, Sunday."

"We'll be back soon, by the Sunday after that, sure. That's when our return tickets are for." Elsie's voice is flat, as if somebody sucked the emotion out her. "Tell Reverend, will ya?"

"Course. So long, Elsie dear."

Our phones click dead.

I wash, too worn out with it all to go through the effort of a shower, and fall into bed. I dream all night. Pale fat, rounded women swim like fish through my dreams. Peacocks with open silent mouths stare. The two men make obscene remarks.

Maybe that's what wakes me, finally, disgusted and bewildered, and tired as I went to bed. Summer heat and humidity seem unbearable. But I still can't take a shower. Can't seem to lift my heavy legs into the tub. It'll have to wait. For what, I'm not sure. Fall and a cool breeze? I shake myself, try to clear my heat-struck head.

This ain't a workin' day, so I take a bus at the corner to the library, not a place I know much about. I've scribbled out on a piece of scratch paper, "Rubens, 1635–37, The Judgement of Paris."

Though it awes me, the library is at least cool. But tombsilent! I take a large breath. There's a clerk at the desk, young and slim. But she smiles at me. When I show her, shyly, my paper, she directs me to another room. "The reference room," she says. "They'll be able to help you."

I wonder.

It's sort of scary, a room full of dark wooden chairs and

tables a few people sit at, books spread before them, some writing busily. At the far end is a desk with an older, skinny woman behind it. I almost turn tail and go, but it's as if there's somethin' magnetic about that postcard full of fat women. I want to know about it.

The woman, when I get brave enough to approach her, not smiling pulls out for me a large book. "Only for use in the library," she says sternly, though surely she can see I ain't gonna try to steal a book *that* size. Particularly bein' *my* size. She offers one smaller book. "You may take this one out if you have a card. And you may look at the other at one of the tables." She is brisk. Her eyes take in my size measuring chairs against my bulk. Oh, I know. "That one in the corner, perhaps?"

Yes, I'll fit, with some squeezing; I can see that. You learn to measure such things.

Everyone, I think, watches me fit myself into the chair. They're not obvious about it, but, as I say, I know. It's been that way since I was sixteen. No, you don't never get used to it.

So here I am, with a big book about, the librarian said, an artist named Peter Paul Rubens. Good biblical names, at least. Perhaps I should talk to Reverend about all this? The smaller book, she said, is on mythology, whatever that is. "The Judgement of Paris is a Greek story, a tale, you see." And she stepped away to answer a demanding phone.

Well, I can tell you, I *don't* see. I can't make head or tail of it all. Why did that biblical painter years and years ago paint a picture about a story older than that, from what I can make out. I pore over the painting, over the short story about the prince named Paris. Was Paris, France, named after him? It's all confusing. How will I explain this to Elsie? I get a headache tryin' to absorb it.

About two P.M. I return the books, thank the librarian (who appears too busy to pay me much attention anyway), and take the bus back to my rooms. It's ninety-two degrees now, by the big thermometer in front of the bank, and humid as hell itself must be.

I hoist myself up the stairs, go to the mantel. Staring at the card I see for the first time that that prince, Paris, is holding a golden apple, just like in the story. Sure didn't notice it last night. But look how it shines like a sun in my shabby room. And, if I was readin' sensibly, those great, fleshy women were goddesses! And beautiful! The painting burns into my eyes, already throbbin'.

I manage to leave it long enough to go to the refrigerator. I get out a whole frozen pizza. I add some Swiss cheese and lunch meats to the top before putting it in the oven. That makes a terrific pizza. I get out some pre-sweetened iced tea and add more sugar to it. I push the last grapefruit juice can to the back of the fridge. That crazy diet, a person could die.

While the pizza is heatin' I think about Mrs. John F. Houston, III. What's it about? Was she being kind, after all, tryin' to make me feel not alone in my fatness? Makin' me feel assured she wouldn't tell Reverend that Elsie and I tipple a bit of the communion wine? But what would be the point of it? Reverend would have laughed, maybe, told us not to, and that would be that, probably.

The oven dinger goes off like a church bell in my head. I pull out the pizza, put it on a platter, place it beside the jug of tea on the kitchen table. I go in, get the postcard, prop it up before me. I eat, eat, hungry, hollow, lost in a strange world of people who do things I can never understand.

How wonderful the pizza is. I savor the strings of cheese, the mushrooms, the anchovies, the rich tomato sauce, the hot frizzled salami I'd added. Wonderful!

They *are* beautiful, the fat pizza-filled goddesses, watched by the handsome prince, and that other man. He's the reverend, I decide, the other man, enjoyin' the whole thing, just like Reverend *would*. The great broad expanses of the ladies are like lights.

They are all me.

The prince, Paris, melts into Mr. Greenwood, bless the man, watching me across the room at a square dance held at another church, long ago, where we met. I didn't square dance; I was much too large for all that skipping and slipping under arched arms, though I was ravenous to fling myself about like the others. Mr. Greenwood, bless the man, my Charlie, hated square dancing, or so he had said as we talked, embarrassed, beside the table piled with grape punch, nice and sweet, homemade cookies, and iced cakes.

That church was set right down in the country. Would I like to walk out in the yard, Charlie had asked, it was such a hot night? I didn't want to leave the cake table; I felt safe there, but I did want to walk with a boy, any boy.

The garden was simple, mostly grass and one bed of roses at the very back. A tangled mass, they almost hid a crumbling wall. That summer the Young People took it on as a project. The night was dark. There weren't no city lights to distract stars from their purposes. Two large maples caught those stars and held them. It was so light, with just the stars, that you could see the sky was a pretty shade of blue tinged with white clouds. We could hear beasts from the farm down the road. The whinny of a horse, the bleat of a lamb, sometimes a dog barking.

At the end of that evening I knew I didn't want to walk with just any boy. I wanted to walk forever with Charlie Greenwood, who worked with his slim, strong hands at building things.

How slowly summers used to pass, like a river that has stopped flowing. There were walks and more walks. Heavy as I was, I loved to walk in the fields that were round us then, down the lanes trees shadowed, Charlie holding my hand, Charlie, at summer's end, askin' me, fat unwieldy me, to marry him.

The phone bell tumbles me back from that summer. I lick my fingers. It is five o'clock already, I see by the cheap cat-shaped clock that hangs on the kitchen wall. I waddle into the front room, pick up the phone.

"Helen," a faraway voice quavers thinly, "Helen, it's Elsie. Listen, Jim's took bad. He's in bed here at his sister's. The doctor says he's not to be moved. I may be here a while, Helen. Jim wanders in his head, but what I can make out, he wants to stay with his family. His other sister came over from Atlanta."

"Geez, Elsie, I'm sorry. Want me to come down?" Though I haven't money to travel with. But I'd get it, somehow, for Elsie.

"Nope. Nothin' you can do, Helen. Just wanted you to know I won't be back for a while. And Jim's family's real good, Helen. It's—nice—to have family." Elsie had none. Same as me, anymore.

"Yeah, it is, for sure, Elsie. Family's real important. I'll tell Reverend on Sunday. We'll all be thinkin' bout you. I'll tell you about bingo, too, when you get back."

"I'll miss communion. No one'll help you wash up, Helen."

"All the more for me." I laugh. Sort of. "You just take care of Jim and yourself, Elsie. We'll talk up a storm when you get home."

"Thanks, Helen. Maybe I'll phone again, if I can."

We say our goodbyes. I clear up, turn on the TV, screen so small I have to squint to see, but there's nothin' that interests me. Fires, murders. Somebody stabbed somebody else, it was still gonna be hot and humid tomorrow....

Nothin' changes. Soon it will be autumn again. No, not now do summers last forever.

I switch to a variety show, people kickin' up lovely long slim legs, singin' songs I can't make out what they're sayin', shoutin' I call it. I snap it off.

It's real hard, but I pull off the clothes that are stickin' to me. And there are my rolls of fat, my white smooth bottom, the great white snowballs of my breasts.

I climb, hard, hard, into the shower and let the needles of water sting me. A long time. At last, needled cool for a while, I labor my way out.

I don't pull on the huge tent of a nightgown I'd stitched for myself. I pull the large armchair right close in front of the table where I prop up, again, Mrs. John F. Houston, III's postcard. A tree by my one window is in full leaf; it shades me from the view of the one neighbor who might see in.

I whoosh down into the chair.

And I walk into the postcard. I am all of them, those great plump goddesses. It is for me that Paris holds out the golden shinin' ball, only it is Charlie Greenwood in the old church garden. He thinks I am beautiful beyond any words he ever found. There's our child, Jeff, playin' in the corner, his pale white skin and golden hair forever young, forever captured in the miraculous garden where we walked. There is Reverend, blessing us, thinkin' (maybe) that my flesh is beautiful. Maybe this Rubens got it all mixed up, this is the original garden where everything was perfect. I don't see no snake, only the golden apple, Charlie, Reverend, and me turned into three goddesses.

Is she mean, Alexandra Houston? Plain mean? One of them people who can't never pass up a chance to dig someone else? Did she pass the painting in that far-off gallery, laugh all silvery to herself, and think, "Oh, I promised Helen Greenwood, poor soul, a postcard, wouldn't it be perfect...?" I want to slip by it, sayin' she *didn't* mean it. I'd like to praise her, but, can I give her that?

Anyway, I'll never tell what she gave me. A place I can walk into anytime I want, with Charlie and Jeff forever with me, Reverend sayin' I'm okay the way I am. And me, myself, repeated, repeated, repeated, big but handsome.

Nope, I'll never tell her. Not me. I ain't got the English to make her understand. So I'll just thank her, tell her how kind she was to remember me, all else she had to do on her trip. Probably I'll tell her, the way I tell Reverend, "Y' done fine, Mrs. Houston."

And *mean* it.

Elsie'll be there to hear me, too. Back in the kitchen, finishin' up the communion wine, Elsie and me'll laugh, not unkindly, but powerful. Kind of holy.

I sit in my armchair a long time. Behind the leaves outside the window the moon's climbin' towards heaven. Full, a great golden apple.

Experiments

They are in the old Esso Station on Mill Street. It now sells some cheap brand of gasoline. Mill Street's a side road on the edge of town. Doesn't get much business.

Why'd they put a station way out there?" Jane's father says. Often, for he doesn't like the filling station downtown whose owner is, he thinks, shifty-eyed. "Can't trust him beyond two minutes from now." But Jane's father continues to go there. He has a minor job at the bank, Jane's father. Lots of prestige (he thinks), little money. He'd *like* to buy the cheaper gas but feels it's not good to be seen there.

Doris and Jane choose the Mill Street station. They are ten years old and friends, sort of. Doris likes to pretend to prefer livelier, better-dressed girls. In fact, she enjoys queening it over Jane, who dotes on her. There are times, lots of times, Doris needs Jane's admiring subservience. It's like getting a fix. She doesn't know that term. Yet.

They are very different. Doris is a plumpish blond whose curls are perfect. She has a candy box prettiness which Jane adores. And envies. Doris smiles a whole lot. Everyone takes to her immediately. Jane can't believe Doris wants her, Jane, for a friend. Jane is skinny, "nothing but brown eyes," her father says, "the whole of her, eyes." He never mentions her commonplace brown hair, straight as a bundle of twigs. Jane thinks about her hair, agonizes over it, especially when she stares at Doris' unflappable ringlets. Don't they *ever* get out of place? Jane thinks about her shyness, too. She is tongue-tied in front of people. Everyone has more important things to say than she. Shyness is a lot like being in prison, she thinks, though she has never been in prison. Nobody brings food or water, either. You just die there, over and over again, famished for words that will make people smile at you, eyes full of favor, as they always do with Doris. Or even angry words. Anything, just so people know you're *there*.

They have carefully locked the women's room door. Doris stands astride the hopper, her panties (pink, lace-edged, expensive; Jane wears cotton ones bought in the supermarket) down around her ankles.

Jane is hanging back, fascinated by Doris' pale, shiny, flawless flesh, scared of it at the same time.

"Come on, hurry. Someone'll want in." Doris bounces her curls towards the rickety door.

Speechless, Jane moves towards her. It is an early fall Friday, a wine-tanged day. It says Jane's feelings, exactly. There is a euphoric sense of beginning again that she always has when fall comes. The dying year? She would not have understood that. Everything seems to begin, after the too-steaming stasis of summer. She loves school, though of course she would never admit that to anyone. She loves the brisk skimming wind through trees, the gem-chip leaves spinning, or lazily drifting, down. An excitement tingles the air.

Just as now, when Jane moves to the silken legs, open like an invitation to a distinctive affair. Not a phrase she knew how to use. No. Open like the hole in the appletree's crotch, at home, where she watched squirrels pop in and out like puppets.

Mesmerized, she places trembling fingers on the rounded plain just below Doris' belly button. It is warm and seems to pulse under Jane's tentative fingers.

"Lower, lower," Doris whispers in the smelly darkness of the women's room. There is only one tiny window, at the top of one wall. It is grimy and shaded by a sad elm tree in the empty lot bordering the filling station.

Their two figures are almost like shadows in the eerie light. There is no electricity. Or at least the bulb has burned out. Each is secretly happy about this; it adds to their sense of stolen mystery. And makes possible what they are about to do. Doris, aggressive, assertive, might have made these maneuvers in the revealing (accusing?) brilliance of glaring light. Jane could never have. Not even for Doris.

Jane's fingers feel as though they are burning, as her face is. They leave the safe plain of the lower belly. They hover uncertainly a moment in the fetid air, then the right hand touches Doris' vulva.

Jane snatches back her hand. Oh, they are burning, her fingers.

"What's the matter?" Doris whispers. "Jane, we must hurry." Her voice trills round the tiny washroom like a small brook. Or so Jane thinks. It draws her on, on, into the current.

Jane's right hand moves forward, slowly, slowly. It is almost stalled in air. Then it finds the lithe vulva again. How inviting it is! Surely it is speaking, Jane thinks. She has, when no one was looking, touched this portion of her doll. It was cold, unyielding. Doris' flesh is like a soft animal. Jane loves animals; she is much closer to them than to people.

She moves her index finger, which is absurdly long, ("You're bound to be a schoolmarm with *that* finger, Jane," her mother laughs as Jane wiggles it at her doll, her cat), pushes aside Doris' labia. The soft folds are—what? Satin? Like the nightgowns she sees in women's magazines, but never wears. And there is a hole. Jane thinks again of the squirrel in the appletree. She gasps.

"Doris, it's—"

"—Exciting!" Doris sighs.

The sigh is like a tiny push, hardly able to be sensed.

Jane moves her long finger into the little hole, oh so gently. In. In. It is, Jane thinks, like the hole down which Alice falls, chasing the White Rabbit. Jane loves *Alice in Wonderland,* has read it twice. Doris struggled through it, for a school book report, and thinks it is a silly book. *Talking lizards, that crazy turtle, playing cards speaking.* Doris stamped her pretty foot in its glossy black patent leather shoe. "Mama thinks it's a ri-dic-u-lous book." Doris' mother is round and plump, like Doris. She adores *art* and *the theater.*

How warm, how beautiful the hole is. Surely, this is Wonderland. The odors here are like nothing she has ever smelled before. Strange fruits, unknown plants. She smiles in the dingy gloom.

It is Doris who appears to be in Wonderland. She is moaning. "Oh, oh, oh, Jane, oh."

Jane's finger suddenly is covered with moisture. Of course, the pool where all the strange creatures swim.

"It's all right," she whispers to Doris. "No one drowns, you know. Remember the story?"

But Doris has reached down, has angrily thrust Jane's hand, the quivering finger, from her.

"What are you talking about?" she hisses. "It was won—*terrible.*" She begins to shiver. "There's something wrong with you, Jane Morville. You're a horrid girl. My mother said so." Doris is crying now. She has jumped from the hopper to the cement floor, almost toppling Jane as she does so.

"You—you asked me to come here," Jane stammers, on the verge of bawling. "You said—"

"No. I never said. You're making it up; my mother says you make up stories all the time. I'm not to play with you anymore."

Jane sobs. "Why did we come here, then?"

"We came because—"

"Come on, you kids." Someone is rattling the door. "You bin in there long enough. Get out."

"Oh," Jane gulps, races for the bolt.

"Wait, wait." Doris pulls up her panties, smooths her dress.

Jane finds an old paper towel on the floor. She doesn't care. Trembling, she wipes off her wet hand, her guilty long finger.

"Out, 'ja hear me?"

The girls blink out into the fresh autumn sunlight.

"Stay away from here, see. Don't want no kids round here." Young Ben Moore slouches off to his office, scowling after them.

"Ben's not quite right. In the head, I mean. My mother says so." Doris picks up her bike, prepares to get on it. They have been stowed behind the filling station, out of sight.

Jane is suddenly tired of what Doris' mother says. She frowns, kicks at a line of colored leaves, and begins to walk her bike towards home.

"Jane," Doris calls after her. "Wait up." Doris has decided to walk her bike, too, conscious still of throbbing where the finger touched her secret center.

Jane stops. A vee of geese follow their long necks high, high above her. How beautiful. Were there geese in *Alice*?

Doris catches up. "I—I can come again after school on Wednesday." Her face is a pale maroon, like the large maple leaf just blowing past her bike. "Can't come tomorrow. I have to go with my mother for a dancing lesson. Ballet," she rattles on, nervously. "My mother says—"

"No." Jane watches the geese become a dot in the sky. "Not Wednesday."

"There's that gas station on Somerset Street, Jane." Doris' golden hair flickers in the sunlight.

How pretty. Jane thinks of her own brown hair, glintless and ordinary. Oh, she is fortunate that Doris wants her to come, wants to be with her. She shuffles her feet. "I—I'll try to come. I might have to go with *my* mother someplace. But," Jane's large brown eyes plead, "your mother says you're not to play with me."

Doris laughs, the extraordinary brook-like laugh Jane loves. "I was teasing, silly. 'Course I can play with you. Wow, it's late." Doris leaps suddenly onto the saddle of her bike and rides off, "Wednesday" trailing back on the wind.

But on Wednesday Doris is not in school. She was in school on Monday and Tuesday, paler than usual, Jane thinks, but looking like a princess in one of Jane's books of fairytales. At recess Doris stayed to help Mrs. Allen with some paperwork. Mrs. Allen, Jane has noted, thinks Doris is a princess, too. Mrs. Allen never notices Jane, except to insist that Jane give a "Formal Talk" in front of the whole class. Mrs. Allen has these talks every Friday afternoon. Turns are taken, by rows. Students are allowed two minutes to give a prepared talk. Two minutes, Jane has discovered, span several lifetimes. She is often absent, *ill*, she tells her mother (and it is hardly a lie) on her Formal Talk day. Mrs. Allen, cordial but narrow-eyed, often makes Jane give her talk the following Monday. Jane dies, each time. She stammers, turns red as her mother's ruffled party dress, and wants, more than anything in the world, to run, howling, into the wood in back of her house, where she will climb the old apple tree and sit where no one can see her. Where she is comforted by, hidden by, welcoming limbs.

At lunchtime on Monday and Tuesday, Doris is whisked off by Marcella Adams and Louise Marks to play leaf houses. Long squares of leaves are lined out on the playground. These are the rooms of the houses. It is a lovely game. Jane is never invited, but she plays it in her imagination. In *her* house there is a bedroom, hers, large and airy, unlike the small cubicle that is hers at home. It is furnished in blues and greens, Jane's favorite colors together. The bed is large and on it sit all Jane's dolls and stuffed animals.

"You're really getting too old for them, Jane, almost eleven. You need to make more real friends." This is what the mother in the imagined house does *not* say. No. *She* buys Jane a small tea set Jane once saw in an antique store, of palest seagreen, rimmed with gold, on which Jane may serve her dolls and animals afternoon tea. Jane is given to, is avid for, English children's stories. It is such an ordered world, in the English Christmas annuals a distant cousin's mother sends her. What would a nursery be like, with a nanny who takes care of you? Jane cannot quite imagine that.

But she can imagine a drawing room with windowseats where she may read on long summer afternoons, and snowy winter ones. The dining room is not one end of the living room, like her real dining room; it is a large, high-ceilinged room hung with a delicious tinkling chandelier. The table is always set with glistening silverware and sky-blue china—thin, thin—on which wander dark blue cornflowers. All is ordered and immensely elegant, just as, Jane is sure, things are in Doris' house, to which Jane has never been invited.

•

Jane watches Doris, Marcella, and Louise work the leaves into squares. Doris makes no sign she knows Jane is watching, half hidden by the oak tree that shadows one corner of the playground. Jane's heart aches at the pale goldenness of Doris.

After school on Tuesday, Doris stays to help Mrs. Allen, again. Jane sees Mrs. Allen stroke Doris' fine, buttery hair. Jane feels her head will burst, maybe her ribs. She runs, runs, all the way home, not seeing the autumn leaves she loves.

At recess on Wednesday, Jane dares to ask Marcella, "Where is Doris Atkins?" in a voice faint with fright.

"Sick. Real sick. Mrs. Allen said her mother called in. "What's it to *you*, Plain Jane?" Marcella scoots to a tightly-knit group of girls who are laughing and combing long, long hair.

Sick? Jane stares at the knot of girls, at the windblown oak tree, at the stern red brick of her school, but what she sees is a dirty, dark washroom on Mill Street, what she hears is Doris moaning, moaning.

What did I do? What did I do?

Jane begins to shake, like the maroon and orange leaves which are, oh yes, are shouting at her. She must go. She must get out of here.

The end-of-recess bell sounds, raucous and threatening. Jane ducks behind the oak tree, watches the other students line up in straggly rows. When the last one has gone in Jane climbs the oak tree. Oh, she has hundreds of times climbed the apple tree near her home, where she goes to be alone, to think and pretend.

Her heart is a tom-tom as she creeps along the long branch extending beyond the forbidding wrought-iron fence which surrounds the playground. Surely her heart will summon AUTHORITIES. She stops, often, to look back towards the brick building, its sun-blazed windows that watch her.

No one comes. Jane stares down at the ground outside the fence. It is a long drop to the ground. Jane sobs, almost falls. Leaves whisper in the breeze, birds scold and taunt: *They'll come after you soon.*

Jane closes her eyes, swings from the branch, a moment, by both hands, then lets go. The thump of her is loud among crackling leaves and twigs, though they have cushioned her fall. She lies, breathless, her heart still a traitor sending messages to the whole world.

Coming, soon, soon, a fat bluejay shrieks. Jane scrambles to her feet. There is a stinging pain in her right ankle, but she can walk. Can run. *Must* run.

The church she comes to is not her own. The one her mother takes her to on occasional Sundays (and always on Christmas and Easter) is a plain whitewashed building where people sing things like "Washed in the Blood of the Lamb," and "By the Old Rugged Cross," and a tall red-moustached preacher roars and whispers, roars and whispers about sin and what sinners we all are. Jane, in the pew beside her father, always sits erect and petrified. Her mother is pleased to see Jane raptly (she thinks) involved. Jane's father, equally upright, in fact can barely keep from snoring aloud.

Jane knows she is a sinner. Her whole body and mind have become weighted with that sure knowledge. That's why she has sped into the first church she comes to.

It is the large stone building on Main Street with a statue of Christ on a cross out front. The Christ is golden, the cross stark white. It stabs the sky. Times she's passed it before, Jane has wondered about that cross. She has never seen a real tree with white wood. Sometimes people in long black gowns move about from the great stone church to a smaller building next door, a school.

There is no time, no time at all to run to her small church on the other side of town.

She has run up the fifteen stone steps oblivious of the paining ankle. She bursts through two finely-carved wooden doors leading from the vestibule into the sanctuary itself. The immense silence stills her. The church appears to be empty. Little candles sit off to one side in a fancy iron rack. Some are burning. Who has lit them?

Jane's hand goes to her open mouth. She has never before seen such a high ceiling. It is full of figures—angels?—in brightest blue and sparkling golds. Their wings are white as the cross holding the bleeding figure outside. The walls are a series of dimly lit niches. Jane inches, on tiptoe, to the first niche. There is a painting of a man with a shaved head and a rough-textured grey—dress? Why is he wearing a dress? What is the bird doing on his shoulder? Why has he that sadly heavy piece of jewelry weighing him down? Small candles flicker in front of the painting, casting long shadows. Oh.

Jane rushes from the niche, slides into a pew almost at the back of the church, tries to make herself invisible. She stares at the tall statue of a woman to the right of a lectern (which seems to be flying in the air), at the front of the church. The woman is wearing a halo like a hat. She looks serenely sad. On the other side of the lectern is another Jesus. *There are drops of real blood on his chest,* Jane thinks, shuddering.

The eyes of all the statues, of all the paintings in all the niches, the eyes of the sad lady and the oozing Jesus stab her with the slitted knives of their narrowed irises.

Sinner, sinner, sinner, the cold mouths whisper, incessantly whisper. *Dirty, dirty child. Sinner, dirty, guilty, sinner, dirty, guilty. Sinnerdirtyguiltysinnerdirtyguilty.* Voices tangle in her hair, sting her bare arms and legs, batter her shaking head, burrow into the echoing chambers of her ears.

Jane's tears flood down the long, twisting roads of her face, splash on her dusty shoes, slide off to the icy stones, where they sit like pebbles on a beach in hell.

Voices, endless voices. *They will all rise, rise like the pack of cards in Alice.* Jane is long past remembering that that was all a dream. No. These cards are knife-edged, will slice her.

She cannot move. She will be here forever, slivers of her scattered on the polished wood of the pew until one of those candles is tossed on her and she turns, burns.

Doris is sick, Doris is dying. Sinner, dirty, guilty, murderer....

Now a sweet, sickly smell enfolds her. It is the smell of that terrible place between Doris' legs, legs that move together, vice-like and permanent.

Come down, Jane sobs to the blue/gold angels, *come down. Please help me, a sinner.*

They float in their starry heaven, remote and passionless.

The little candles sputter and wink. Jesus bleeds from his dark wounds, the lady stares at an unseen vision.

Jane's tattle-tale heart raps out messages unheard in the splendid sanctuary, the terrifying tumbling-on world.

The next morning, a bouncing radiant fall morning, they find her, pallidly, almost imperceptibly, alive, her face scratched by frantic nails, tiny clumps of her hair pulled out and lying like threads stained blue by sun through stained glass.

Later, in the stern white hospital bed, where does she go in the unknown avenues of delirium? Does part of her float to another dimension, trying to reunite with the strange, lost, raving one?

"What could have possessed her?" Jane's mother frowns over her daughter, still in an uneasy sleep.

"God," a thin night nurse nods knowingly. "She's always calling for God." The nurse resolves to bring in a silver cross for the girl to wear. Like a charm.

"God?" Jane's mother pulls at a dark hair growing from her chin.

So the red-moustached preacher is asked to come in the next afternoon. He comes to Jane's bedside, puts his hands on her thrashing ones, and thunders "Peace, sister."

Jane wrestles her hands loose. Wild-eyed, she screams at him, cannot stop. Shaken, and shaking his head, he leaves, murmuring, with eyes rolled towards heaven, "Possessed."

Jane weeps, relentlessly, flowing into herself to the place where there is nothing. And no one.

The Summoning

The small resort town of Portstewart, Ireland, is built on two levels. The upper is dotted with homes, villas, boarding-houses that perch on the low hills. The lower level is the promenade, busy and lively with shops: a grocery store, a meat monger, a tourist shop full of crosses, wishing wells, and figures carved out of black bog oak, postcards of the beauti-ful Coast Road that runs round the whole northern coast of Ireland, several little restaurants, and so forth. The two levels are connected by a set of long, narrow stone steps, worn down in the centers by thousands and thousands of feet pass-ing from one level to the other. You *can* go way around on a road, but the steps are more direct, if more wearing.

On a typical half-rainy, half-sunny day, a day when wind pushed puffy clouds into continually changing shapes, Frances Allen parked her small rented car away down at one end of the promenade, slid from behind the wheel, locked the doors, and drew in a deep spring breath.

May in the British Isles. Lovely.

A time to forget, for a while, all one's small anxieties and complexities.

Frances checked her tote bag. Yes. A book, her writing pad, pencils. Taking up the tote bag and her handbag, she started along the promenade, just under the high stone wall of a convent that rode the headland beside the long "front." Frances stopped a moment to look up at the rather forbid-ding-looking wall. They had told her, back at the Information Center, that you could walk right round the perimeter of the convent, the North Sea dashing up against the thick wall the whole way.

"A pleasant walk," the tourist office people had said.

She'd come back to that, Frances decided. Now she terribly wanted a cup of morning coffee, and after it, wanted to wander in and out of the little shops before settling somewhere with her book, her writing pad, to enjoy a lazy afternoon.

Resisting several shops on the way, resisting the call of the thrashing North Sea roaring against the walls of a picturesque small harbor at one end of the front, Frances went into the first small teashop she came to. She'd driven for two hours up from Belfast, had started early, wanting the whole day here. She was, after all, on a kind of mission. What does sleep matter when you are on a mission *and* a holiday, when you are a fetchingly pretty lemon-haired twenty-four-year-old, and when you don't want to miss one single thing? Sleep, Frances thinks, is for the old.

The teashop was done all in yellow and white, rather like the daffodils ravishing on the hills as she drove in. A canary sang in a cage at the rear. Absorbing its joy, Frances took a tiny table next to the window overlooking the front and the sea.

"Yes, that's all right, miss," a middle-aged waitress smoothed her yellow apron and nodded as Frances looked questioningly at her. "May be a rush a bit later, but now anywhere you want is fine." She smiled, pushed back a wandering wisp of greying hair. "Out from America, eh? On holiday?"

"Yes. How did you know? I hadn't said a word." Frances laughed.

"Oh, your lovely clothes, miss, and—I don't know, an air.... Will you have tea?"

"Coffee, I think, though I do love your good Irish tea. Coffee and one of those sugar buns, please."

"Right away, miss." The waitress moved off. Frances looked down at her ultrasuede sky-blue outfit, shoes to match, bought just for this trip. Were they really so distinctive, so foreign? Never mind. What odds. She lit a cigarette. No "No Smoking" signs here, thank God. She was tired, at home, of being made to feel guilty every time she just wanted a puff or two. Wasn't it her own business if she died of lung cancer, or something?

She looked out at the front, now a bit more crowded. Mothers with prams, a boy with his fishing pole and box going towards the snug harbor, women doing morning shopping, retirees muffled against the wind, out to sit on one of the benches to watch the endless movement of the sea.

I'll have to find a real estate agent, I suppose, she thought. *That place near where I parked the car's as good as any, probably.*

Frances *had* come partly on holiday, but she had heavier reasons for having quit her executive secretarial job and taken off for Ireland.

"Take a leave of absence, Frances. You're a fine secretary; the job can let you go for a short while," her boss was kind enough to say when she told him she was leaving.

"No, thank you very much, Mr. Harper, but I want to make a complete break. May go back to school to become a lawyer. I've been saving; I'd like a real profession."

"You have the brains, surely. I admire your ambition, Frances, though I'll be done out of a first-class secretary, and believe me, that's a rare commodity these days. Most can't spell, and that's the least of it."

So she had made her arrangements, and here she was.

She had a lot to think about.

What she had *not* told Mr. Harper was that she was summoned here.

"Summoned? By whom? A relative, you mean?" She could see his odd look, his non-understanding, had she mentioned such a strange thing.

And she couldn't possibly have told him about the voice in the night.

It was a woman's voice. No, certainly not a relative's. She had no relatives here now. At the age of two she had emigrated from here with her parents. For some years they kept in touch with several distant cousins, but they were gone now.

It didn't come every night. Mostly, it awakened her on windy nights, almost as if the trees themselves were whispering. She had gone to her bedroom window the first time she heard the voice, to see trees tossing, leaves rubbing against each other. Was that what sounded so like a human voice?

But it wasn't the trees.

It was, yes she felt almost sure, the voice of a woman, a high, melodious voice that rose and fell like a line of music, now forte, now pianissimo. At first she couldn't make any sense of what it seemed to be saying. Then as, half frightened, half fascinated, she listened carefully, she made out the words *Come, come to Ireland. Come home, come home.*

The full moon shattered in the tangle of swaying trees. In the distance a cat yowled.

Startled by that reality, Frances had slammed shut the window, raced, shivering, back to her warm bed. *What was happening to her mind?* She was not given to fancy, to hearing odd voices.

Too frightened even to get up to take a sleeping pill, she huddled, awake, all night, her mind racing.

Brilliant sunlight made her ashamed. What nonsense. She wouldn't have a pizza loaded with everything just before bedtime again. Tired out, but revived a bit by daylight, she dressed, went to work, resolutely putting the incident out of her mind.

The whole family came to her mother's and father's house for Thanksgiving that year: an aging aunt, a brother and his wife and two children, two sisters, their husbands, four children between them. After a far-too-laden table they gathered in the living room around a leaping fire. Talk fell, as it often did with them, to reminiscing.

"It was lovely, Portstewart. We were there on holiday for a whole summer. You don't remember it, of course, Frances."

"No." *Of course not.* They knew she didn't. Why did they always mention it?

"Heathmount Gardens is where you were born. A tiny house in a row, up on the hill. What fun we had running down all those narrow steps to the sea."

They went on and on. Frances sat, assuming an interest, seething, feeling, as she often did, as though she really did not belong in this family. Had they adopted her and never told her? All those Irish tales about stolen babies. Did she really belong somewhere else?

"You ought to go and see it someday, Frances. Take a holiday in Ireland, find the house. Wouldn't it be fun to see where you were born?"

"Yes, great fun," Frances smiled obediently. "Perhaps I'll manage it some day."

The idea had taken hold. If she saw the reality, perhaps she wouldn't feel so like an outsider anymore. Perhaps they'd shut up about her not remembering.

She began to save in earnest after that, doing without this and that, skipping lunches. When she finally landed the job with Mr. Harper, where she ran the one-girl office, she began to make good money. Mr. Harper's business, based on his own patents, was hugely successful. To his credit, he appreciated Frances and paid her well. She knew she was giving up a good thing when she told him she was leaving for good. *But if I change my mind,* she had thought, *I think he'd take me back,* though she felt deep in her bones that she was leaving for good. There were other worlds to be explored.

Through all the making of travel plans, buying a few new clothes, the voice did not stop. Always on a windy or rainy night there was the woman summoning her.

Frances decided, finally, that it must be a projection of her own intense wishes and desires. Some part of her that wouldn't let her forget her goal when, occasionally, she began to think it might be more interesting to go, say, to Italy.

Come home, come home, the voice would say, wet trees slapping the message against her window. *Come to Ireland.*

And Frances, who thought herself to be totally American, knew there was in her some of the Irish mystic, after all. Genes were not to be denied.

Here she was, then, in Ireland, in Portstewart, having coffee on the front on a radiant May morning, about (she hoped) to find the house where she was born.

"Sugar and cream, miss?" the waitress put down before her a large bun.

"No, neither, thanks. By the way," Frances had a sudden inspiration, "do you happen to know where a place called Heathmount Gardens is?"

"Aye, right up at the top of the steps and across one road. You know the steps between the two levels?"

Frances nodded.

"Five minutes from here. Do y'know someone there, dearie?"

"No. My mother used to know someone there, that's all." Frances sipped her coffee.

"Ah well, take a look for your ma's sake, there's a good girl." The waitress put down a check, moved to a table where a boy and girl were staring moonily into each other's eyes.

Frances didn't hurry. The view was lovely, gulls shrieking and dipping, men in the harbor mending nets, sea rearing up against the sea wall. And now she hadn't to find a real estate agent, she could dally a little. She sipped, stared.

Surely it couldn't have changed a great deal since her family spent a summer here, the summer she was born. By straining forward she could see again the convent and its seawalk and wall. How many times she had heard her sisters tell of running round it, teasing the nuns. Well, she would see it for herself, all in good time.

She finished the last of her bun—so sticky, so good—had a second cup of coffee, then washed her sticky hands in the little cloakroom in the rear.

Fortified, she went to the long, narrow steps that connected the two parts of the town. She paused a minute at the bottom, waiting for two young boys to half tumble down, their footsteps echoing on the stone, hitting off the narrow walls. She peered up the steps. She thought she could see her sisters, her brother, giggling, pushing each other down the steps, could see her mother coming with her market bag, her father with his fishing rod.

Shaking her head to clear it, she began the long, steep climb, conscious at every step that she was treading where her family had trod. There was an eeriness to it, a sense of time not having passed at all. What was time, anyway? Weren't they here, children as they had been? Those adults in America were other people. Yes, she was sure of it. It was a revelation to her. You didn't just grow up, grow old. You left yourself at other stages in other places, alive, sentient. Her mother was still a girl in Donegal, her father a callow boy in Clonis.

The sun was just past full noon when she emerged, dazed, at the top of the steps. White lamb-like clouds formed delicious shapes, hurrying across the sky. She paused a moment to look round her. There was the one road the waitress had mentioned. A few cars ran along it. Frances crossed it. There before her was a tattered sign: HEATHMOUNT GARDENS.

"No. 5; it's No. 5 I'm looking for." Frances was not conscious of having spoken aloud.

"No. 5 Heathmount? Third in, miss, just there." An old man with a dog pointed.

Such a small row house it was, ivy half covering its blue-painted front. The garden before the house was small, a tangle of daffodils, tulips, wild primrose, and coarse green grass badly in need of mowing.

What had she expected? She'd been told it was a row house, just a summer stop. Why the feeling of disappointment then? She swallowed the learned lesson: the romance in the mind is always greater than the reality.

The front gate to the little yard was latched. Slowly she undid it, walked up the overgrown path to the house, its peeling door. She rang the bell, not really expecting anyone to answer. It looked deserted, unkept. *And her family was gone.*

But there was a fumbling on the other side of the door. Shortly a child, a toddler—one and a half, two, two and a half—Frances wasn't good at judging kids' ages—appeared at the not even half-opened door. She had blond short curls and was pale, as if even the rare British Isles sun had not touched her sufficiently. Her eyes were brown and very large. She didn't speak.

"Er—may I, that is, is your mother in?" Frances asked.

The child shook her head in a slow negative.

"Are you alone? Is there a sister at home perhaps?"

"Later," the child said. The door creaked shut.

111

Frances was baffled. *Damn.* She wanted to see the house, to see the parlor where (she had been told) the upright piano used to stand, to see the room where her own crib must have been.

Later.

The child must mean her mother would be back in a short while. Who would leave a small child alone for very long, or at all, in fact? She stood for a minute or two, uncertain as to how to proceed. The lace curtain in the front room moved a little as she watched. Was the child peering out at her? No, the wind, probably, for the window was open. There was nothing to do but try later. Maybe the mother was down on the front with her market basket and wouldn't be long.

Frances walked slowly down the rough garden path to the gate. Outside the gate she leaned against the stone wall and, trembling, lit a cigarette. It was ridiculous, really, to have come three thousand miles on the strength of a whispery voice which might well have been the wind. Wasn't it?

No. It was more than that. It was so that she could say at the next family gathering, with a knowledgeable air, "Oh yes, a small house in a row, but looking out to sea at least, and pert daffodils and primroses in the garden, too."

She would think no more about it, would go back down to the front, find a bench and read or write in the beautiful May sunlight.

She looked back at the house. The window curtain undulated slightly. All else was still.

She went rapidly down the long steps, walked out onto the sea wall, loving the spray tossed up on her face, the hammering waves, and, on the other side of the wall, the quiet harbor full of all manner of boats. A gull—how large they were close up—settled a foot from where she stood on the sea-wet wall. Sunlight stroked it, made golden its keen eyes. At last, seeing she had nothing to offer, it flew off, shrieking.

Frances moved back to the now-crowded front. She was lucky enough to find an empty bench, where she settled herself with her book, a vacation thriller. She opened it, but was too entranced with the scene around her to concentrate.

What a lovely little town, despite the child's disappointing reception.

I'll stay the night here, if I can, Frances decided, delighted with sun, sea, birds, the busy, yet somehow peaceful, promenade, the hills, the ever-changing clouds.

She had come to Ireland simply to wander at will, as long as her money held out, after fulfilling her original mission: to see where she was born. Yes, she must spend one night here.

After an hour or so she made her way to a place near her carpark advertising ROOMS TO LET. A clean, pleasant woman showed her a room looking right out onto the sea; it was available for one night. Frances took it, said she'd bring in her bag after a bit, indicating where her car was parked.

"Aye, it's safe there. Anytime you want to come in will be fine. You've your own key. We don't lock the front door at night. Enjoy the rest of the day, my dear."

Frances could have kissed her. There was the welcome she had been hoping for. She beamed at the woman, Mrs. Ball, thanked her, and made for the convent wall walk, leaving her tote bag in her room jaunty and bright with primroses and whin.

The walk, when she climbed up to it, appeared to be new, not the old narrow one her sisters used to talk of. It was, too, surprisingly high above the water and rocks below. It had not looked quite so massive from the front. Trees growing inside the convent grounds overhung the walk in places, dappling the path with shadows. Old leaves from the previous fall huddled together in a few dark corners. There was almost no-one on the path. Frances passed two boys on bicycles and one young woman in a running outfit. She saw no nuns. It was a lovely walk; Frances felt that some of the peace she imagined existed inside the cloistered walls spilled out in front of her as she walked, lightening her path. There were benches at intervals. She sat down on one, wishing she had brought her book, after all. But once more sun, sea, and spring seduced her. She wouldn't have read much at any rate, she knew.

A dog trailing his lead came briskly along. Soon after, a

middle-aged man, puffing, tried to catch him. Frances closed her eyes, listened to the sea below hitting immense rocks, receding, shifting endlessly. She must have dozed; when she opened her eyes the sun was far down the sky and she was, suddenly, hungry.

She made her way back the long walk, down steps, to the front. Earlier, she'd noticed an inviting-looking restaurant. She went in, ordered prawns, beef-and-kidney pie, a salad, a sweet and good red wine. American pop music played in the background, but softly, unobtrusively. Frances watched the sun sink, sink, ah a long while in the stretched Irish twilight, into the sea. The wine made her drowsy. The bright little room with its clean bed began to seem attractive to her. She finished the last of her wine, paid her bill, and left.

Slowly she walked to her boarding house, among long shadows reaching out into the sea. Sandcastles built earlier in the day slipped back to their beginnings, birds found their nightly roosts. Laughter and the clink of glasses spun out of a little pub she passed. She saw the waitress who had served her morning coffee sitting beside a man whose hand rested knowingly on her substantial knee.

Frances got the small bag out of her car, locked up again and went to the second floor, where her room was. In minutes she was in a hot bath, with good thick fluffy towels at hand to receive her afterwards.

She felt totally at peace, totally at home. Roots were important to seek out, to find, never mind if they sometimes had an unpleasant growth or two on them.

There was a television set. She tried to watch late news but was too sleepy. Opening her window wide to the loved sound of the sea, she got in between clean scented sheets and in minutes was asleep.

Come home, come home.
Frances woke, confused. Where was she?

Consciousness flooded back. She was in Ireland; there were no trees just outside her window, as in America, that might whisper and murmur.

Completely awake now, she sat up in bed, listening. The voice came through the open window full of moonlight.

Come home, come home....

"But I *am* home," Frances said aloud. What did it mean, the insistent voice? She had followed it across the Atlantic to this place, after all. Or was it wind over the rocks she was hearing?

Come, come. Was there a figure in the bright moonlight? She was not sure. The voice was as melodious as ever, singing its remembered tune. It was lulling, like a mother calling to her child.

Frances got up. Half entranced by the moon, the sea's whinings, and the song, she pulled on her clothes, unlocked her door, the voice always just before her, calling, calling, soft as a butterfly's flutter.

There was no one about as she went down the steps and out onto the promenade. The pub had closed long since. Moonlight sat on deserted benches, made shop signs glow, sparkled the sea, the little harbor, the bobbing boats, filled the holes in stretched-out fishing nets.

How beautiful it was.

Wings of light went on before her. Frances followed, unafraid. This was a voice she knew, no stranger in the bright washed night.

She followed up the steps to the convent walk, easily, not toiling as she had earlier.

Come home, come home.

The will o'the wisp light floated on before her.

At a clearing where she could stand and look right down onto the light-brushed rocks jutting out of immense swells of sea, the light stopped.

Then the light billowed again before her, now in the shape of a woman whose form Frances could see right through to the sea, the stones, the shadows.

"Who—who are you?" Frances managed to whisper.

"The banshee, of course, dear. What a long way I had to travel to find you, to make you come home, here where you belong." The voice was light as a far-off bird's.

Frances put her hand to her mouth, out of which no sound would come.

The figure before her, willowy, lovely in moonlight, wavered like a candle in wind. As Frances watched, it changed. It was a child, she could see, straining, squinting. A child with blond curls, pale, pale skin, and immense brown eyes.

"You always knew, didn't you, that you didn't belong with them?"

Agile, lithe, the child stepped, floated, over the edge of the unguarded cliff, "Come home" trailing after her like bubbles of seaspray.

And Frances followed the siren song of the child into the mothering arms of the sea.

Blood Rites

"I don't want to go," Anna whispers to her mother after her father has left the kitchen. Although she hears his step creaking up to his study, she is afraid that he may hear her resistance.

"Nonsense, Anna. You enjoy fishing. He enjoys company. I can't go because of my students' recital. Pack a few things like a good girl and don't keep your father waiting. I'll fix a thermos of coffee and some sandwiches; that way you'll save buying dinner. You'll have only breakfast to pay for tomorrow morning."

"But—"

But Mrs. Carter has hurried to fetch the picnic basket from the basement cupboard. Anna's syllable floats round the kitchen, full of summer air and flower scent, like a bee waiting to light.

I won't, won't go. Anna's thought matches the stamp of her foot. Dust motes mingle with early afternoon sun-motes. Anna feels she can hear them bump and explode. Bump, bump, bump. Maybe it is her heart?

Won't sleep near him all night in the car. *Why, I've just got my period.* Her face flushes at the thought of that sticky flow, still so new to her. *How will I change, suppose it leaks through and he sees it, I'll die for sure.* I can't go.

"Anna!" Mrs. Carter's voice jolts. "Still standing here? Run; I'll have the sandwiches packed in a minute. Dad's fishing things are ready. He fixed them last night. *Fly.*"

"Why can't we sleep in two rooms near the beach? One of those cheap little houses?"

"You know perfectly well why, child. Because they're not cheap enough. My dear, we simply haven't the money." Mrs.

117

Carter's face softens. Wouldn't it be nice to say "Get two rooms at a hotel. Order your breakfast sent up in the morning?" But such luxuries are not the lot of an assistant professor of English with five children. She doesn't make much giving a few piano lessons. "One of these days when your father gets his promotion...."

"Sure." Anna sighs; she has heard it before.

In her room she filches from a drawer all the panties she owns, puts on two pair and two pair of shorts. Why hasn't she *any* dark-colored ones? She tosses into her gym bag a denim skirt. No bathing suit. And Dad will, she imagines, ask her why she isn't going for a swim. *Oh, I won't go!* But her sisters and brothers are working; she is the only child free to go. She kicks her bedpost, picks up her gym bag, and stomps downstairs.

The ride to the shore is uneventful. Anna is, almost, used to Dad's erratic style of driving. If there is a patch of scenery he likes, he ambles along discoursing on the flora, holding up a line of traffic. When the line of cars, finally, passes him, he's like a foxhound given the scent. His foot thumps down on the gas pedal and they're off on the chase.

To get to the remote, sparsely-populated island where Dr. Carter likes to fish they must cross a high bridge which seems to Anna to sway. Anna peers down, down, interested in spite of herself. The sea below, shadows of birds on it like other, smaller islands. *I love it, I love the ocean.* If she could just sleep on the beach. Alone.

They park just beside the fishing pier, which stretches far out into the Atlantic. At water's edge, Anna thinks, another world begins. *I'll cross it someday, to Scotland.* She has been reading the romantic novels and poems of Sir Walter Scott. Why couldn't she have lived then, in the midst of wild winds and extraordinary people instead of—

"Now if you'll help me carry things out to the pier, Anna, I'd be grateful." Her father's ordinary voice punctures her reverie.

"Of course." Anna picks up a small folding stool. Her father takes rods, tackle box, and bait, after locking the car, its trunk stuffed with blankets and two pillows for the night.

At four in the mid-summer afternoon the pier is moderately crowded with fishermen and women. People nod as Anna and her father trek to the very end. Caught fish flop in pails of seawater, sun glints on a tin-topped table with running water where several men gut their catch. Scales wink and glitter. Lines swing out, hooks and bait flashing before plopping to depths Anna cannot imagine. A fishy smell pervades everything, but it isn't unpleasant. It's clean. Anna thinks of splendid creatures washed in the long sweep of the sea. She watches gulls hover and sink to clusters of guts, then rise up to their screaming companions. A few sit on the sea like toy boats.

"Stay and watch if you want, Anna, or run to the beach and have a swim. You've time before we have Mother's sandwiches. It won't be dark for a long while."

Dark! In the confusion, glitter, and leaping life of the pier, Anna has forgotten dark and what it will mean: her bedding down in the back seat of the car while Dad somehow curls his long frame into the front, his eventual snoring, her shivering fear—of what?—so that she will not, she's sure, sleep. *Oh, let dark never come.*

"I'll—I'll watch for a while," she murmurs. But her father is already absorbed. She's afraid to ask for a rod and reel, afraid the jerk of her arms and body, casting, will cause a flood, there, in front of everybody.

She watches for a while, mesmerized by sun, whining lines, the silence except when someone reels in a catch. But there's nowhere to sit, except on a hard bench. Mild cramps make her hunch; she will have to find a women's room and change the pad.

It's easy to get the keys from her father, distracted by sport. She roots in her bag for a clean pad, carefully wraps it in a brown paper bag she brought, so no one will guess what it is.

The women's room is primitive but private. She tosses the bloody pad—how odd, that her blood should drain so easily away—into a pail and decides to walk on the beach.

She takes off her sandals, lets small waves rush over her feet, cooling her. It is *hot*, ninety-two degrees, Dad said. She bends, fascinated, over a dead king crab. Isn't it magnificent? Could she gut it and mount that beautiful shell in her room? She pokes at it, lifts it with a stick; the odor makes her back away. Shells, iridescent, dazzling, lie everywhere. She picks up several for her collection at home. Driftwood, some pieces burnished by the sea, some roughly handsome, holds summer air. Have all these things roamed round from Scotland's coast? For a long while she is lost in the land of pretend.

"Awk." A gull (how large they are!) whooshes down beside her. Anna blinks, looks at the sun. She must get back to the pier. She buckles on her sandals and runs, awkwardly, too conscious of the pad holding her life's blood.

"It's past seven, Anna," her father says, mildly. She is panting. "You must have had a good long walk. Look," he points at his pail, "two croakers and a flounder. It's been a splendid afternoon. And I'm ravenous, aren't you?"

"Yes," Anna says, and discovers that she really is. "What'll you do with the fish, Dad?"

"Hm." He frowns. "Maybe the man in the coffeeshop will freeze them until we leave tomorrow. He's done it before if things aren't too crowded."

The man agrees to keep the fish overnight, for a dollar. Soon they are sitting at a wooden table on the shore portion of the pier, eating Mrs. Carter's cold turkey and ham sandwiches, with creamy steaming coffee from the thermos. Hot coffee tastes yummy even in the hottest weather. Anna wouldn't have given a dime for a cold soda.

"I'm going to fish a bit more, Anna; the fishing's fine at twilight, usually. Did you bring a book?"

"Yes." Anna rarely goes anywhere without a book. "I'll be all right, Dad. Don't worry about me." She knows he won't, caught in the mystique of fishing. She opens her book but finds the pier, with its different evening sounds and lights, intriguing. Too, she can't put out of her mind the night to come. She shivers. What *is* she afraid of? She decides to concentrate, hard, on the gulls. She follows a single gull with her eyes for a long time. It dips, sinks, flares up, squabbles. She begins to spin in her head a tale about where it lives, what kind of family it has, where it goes to sleep for the night....

Her *own* night is suddenly upon her. Here is her father, fishless but jaunty.

"Time to bed down, Anna. The gulls and surf will wake us early."

She trails after him, carrying the stool. She tosses it into the trunk when her father pulls out the bedding, wishing she could sit up on it all night, down at surf-edge, listening to the sea's comfort.

"Won't they make us leave, Dad?" she ventures hopefully as he puts blankets and one pillow into the back seat for her.

"No; they're lenient about fishermen here. The one night pier guard knows me."

But aren't there police? Surely, surely, the police will make them go. She can't bring herself to say this aloud, afraid her voice will break and her father will say, "Now what on earth are you crying for, child, a lovely evening, a little holiday, a comfortable place to sleep. Many would be glad of it."

"I'll go wash my teeth," is all she can manage. She seizes her gym bag.

"Good; I'll do the same." Her father walks beside her, distant as the moon just slipping up the sky.

The women's room is, fortunately, deserted. Anna, clutching her bag of shame, hurries to do the necessary.

Soon they are settled, she in the back seat, he in the front.

"Sleep well, little Anna. My, sun and air make one drowsy, eh?"

"Mm," she murmurs, pretending to be already almost asleep.

Her father has hung towels at the windows, for darkness. He manages to crack one window open for air, turned surprisingly chill. Anna gulps it in, frantically.

The heavy animal smell of her father fills the car as if it were a lair. His snores, rather delicate, like strange bells, sound on her flesh, chime into her bones.

Will he come in the night and touch her?

Anna thrusts a fist into her mouth to stifle sobs. *That is it, then, the fear that has gnawed at the edges of her mind and heart all day.* Now she has named it. Will his fingers, patrician, out-of-place-looking on a fishing rod, find the small buds of her breasts, move to the hidden belt, the soaked pad? Men do things like that. Mary Allen, at school, has told Anna about *her* father's fumblings, nights her mother goes to Bridge Club.

A small scream escapes her. The snoring stops. "All right, Anna?" Sleepily.

"Yes, oh, yes," she gasps, covering her mouth with both hands until the snoring begins.

The night full of shadows moves on. A door slaps shut somewhere. A bird whines. Small clouds slip across the barely visible moon.

Anna lies rigid. The pungent smell of her own sex rises like a wild live thing. It will wake him, surely, and then, and then....

One of the towels begins, rhythmically, to tap at the window. Slap-slap, slap-slap. Anna slips to restless sleep. A gull comes to nip at her breast. The king crab walks upright, hollow shell like a pale ghost on a black beach. Fish scales whirl like sleet, hitting, stinging.

"Anna, child, you're shivering like a sapling in a high wind. Now then, wrap yourself up in my blankets for a bit before we go to the shop for good hot coffee."

"Coffee?" Anna chatters. "But the crab, the gull." She bolts upright. "What's that light?"

"Early dawn, Anna. Light—and lovely. Want to see it out on the beach?" He has put his blankets round the shivering girl as he talks.

"But—but—in the night—*you didn't touch me!*" Anna blurts out.

"Touch you?" Dr. Carter stares. His face suddenly seems older. "Is that what you—?" He stops, pulls on a sweater. "Come, Anna," He says quietly. "Let's watch sun-up."

"I—I—" Anna is unable to stop stuttering, shivering. "The lavatory—I must—"

"Yes. I know." He is grave. "Take your gym bag and the blankets. I will meet you on that washed-up log. Just there." He points to the right of the pier. "It's all right, Anna. No one will disturb you." He opens the car door for her.

Can she get out, she wonders? Will blood stream down her legs, giving her away? Are the blankets already a rust-colored mess?

Her father's back is towards her, his hand at his eyes fixed on the ocean.

She struggles out of the car, out of sleep, the clammy, sodden pad like a weight. Stumbling, clutching the gym bag, she goes to the lavatory where she heaves the contents of her churning stomach into the cold white porcelain hopper.

But nothing has leaked! The blanket has no stains, though her inner panties do.

Trembling, she throws them into the waste bin, pulls on two more pair and the jeans skirt, after changing the pad, white as a gull, new as morning.

She takes long, deep breaths, pulls the blankets round her again, and goes to meet her father at the log.

"Think of it, Anna," her father begins as if resuming an ongoing conversation. "The sun comes up like that every morning." Suddenly he says, slowly, "'The blood turns in my veins! Away, O soul! Hoist instantly the anchor! Cut the hawsers—haul out—shake out every sail!—Darest thou now, O soul, walk out with me toward the unknown region where neither ground is for the feet nor any path to follow?'"

Anna stares. What is he talking about?

"That was Whitman, Anna, one of America's greatest poets. A man for daring unknown regions. As you've dared to walk this one with me. You've been very brave." He turns to face her, carefully does not touch her hand, though he would like to clasp it in his.

Anna looks at the sun laying a path on the sea. "I don't understand. I just came on a fishing trip with you."

"An unknown region, wasn't it? One that—didn't it?—scared you terribly. Poor child-becoming-a-woman," he says, almost to himself.

Anna bites her lip. "I wasn't *really* scared, it was just—"

"Fathers are sometimes fools, Anna." He bends, tosses a shell towards water. "But," he turns back towards her, "there's more to it. Another great poet said, 'As contagion of sickness makes sickness, contagion of trust can make trust.' Sometimes you have to trust people, Anna. Sometimes you even have to trust fathers, those great blundering oafs."

Anna almost laughs. Shyly. "You're—you're not an oaf."

"Not always, maybe. See that gull? It trusts air to hold it, though the air appears not to care."

"It's moving on a path towards Scotland." Anna has shaken off the blankets. The sun is warm, magnificent.

"To Scotland? Well, perhaps. That path leads home again, too. Which is where girls of thirteen ought to sleep, not in a cramped car with an aging father."

"It—it wasn't so bad." Anna swallows. Hard.

"Dear Anna. Smell fresh coffee? Let's get some." He gathers the blankets and starts off.

Anna watches the sunpath, the color of blood—what had her father quoted: "blood burns in my veins"? He'd made it sound—well—*dignified*. And said she had courage!

"Trust me, Anna, trust me." Her father's voice floats back. "A young lady named Anna is going to have a breakfast fit for a queen."

Anna remembers, or was she dreaming?, the animal smell of her father in the dark. The pungent odor of her own blood flails her nostrils; it is ancient as the musk of creatures, not yet quite human, in the cave.

She runs to water's edge, flings off her sandals, wades in the cleansing sea.

A gull drifts just above the water. Will it dip to the dense sea world or climb the sunwashed air? Anna stares, her bare feet numbing, until the gull steps up to the blue and white rooms of sky. Up, up.

Only then does she turn, feet tingling, towards her father's voice, towards life, its sure uncertainties.

Sunday Morning Bells

It lay in a puddle of moon in the back yard near the bird feeder. The boy almost kicked it aside, thinking it was a stone. But a slight movement held his foot in suspension a moment before he planted it several inches away from the blob of brown.

"Why, it's an animal," he said near a great sycamore whose leaves, windblown, let the moonlight through in swaying patterns. The boy knelt to the small thing. He saw that its sides were barely pumping in and out, though there were no marks on it that he could see.

"Where'd you come from?" His breath was soft, as if it could blow away the tiny thing. The hardly-more-than-pin-size eyes opened briefly. The boy saw terror in them. They shut. Fast. He took out a dirty handkerchief and carefully moved the tiny body onto it.

"What will I do with you now?" he mused as the moon disappeared slowly, slowly, behind the thicket of leaves.

Behind him, some twenty yards away, the back door to the great white house sat grandly in light from the handsome lamp set over it, lit against whatever darkness might try to slither in. The door was of solid oak, varnished to bring out the fine grain. The house was of Civil War era, quite majestic and haughty. It was full of shadows.

The boy hesitated. The Great Lady who was his mother would make short shrift of the morsel he could feel palpitating through the hankie in his hand. The Great Gentleman who was his father would knock his pipe against the fireplace and pierce him through with eyes able to cut a balance sheet down to size in a trice.

It was time to go in. The summer evening had drifted

away two hours ago; it was now officially night. He would be expected.

He looked at the lighted door, frowned, and set off for the large maple tree beyond the hedge enclosing the formal garden where he now was. Once there, he hesitated again. How was he going to climb the tree without killing the small creature? After some thought he twisted the four corners of the hankie together, and managed to tuck the twisted tops into his belt. It was the best he could do. Gently as light touching a leaf, he climbed up, up to his treehouse hidden away in the arms of the tree.

The "house" was just one small room with one not-quite-square window shut against weather with a tacked-up piece of plastic. An orange crate begged from the local market served as a seat, another as a table. A blanket Angelina, the maid, had given up *(What are you up to? Missus'll have my skin.* But she had let him have it, a half smile notching the corners of her wide mouth) was thrown over the seat-crate.

The boy pulled off the blanket, whirled the crate upside down. He stuffed the blanket into one side.

"Like a nest, like a *home,*" he told the small totem pole that stood against one wall. The boy had made the totem pole in Indian Guides. Crooked and rough though it was, it was a friend he often talked to.

He slipped the handkerchief from his belt, untied it, and peered by flashlight, kept on the crate-table, at the quaint figure which now looked almost dead. He lowered it onto the center of the blanket.

—It must have food—said the totem pole.

—Food! Yes, yes, but I don't know what to feed it—

—You must get an eyedropper and warm milk. All babies like warm milk—

—So they do. Maybe Angelina...?—

—Yes—

The boy studied the wee pulsing thing for a few more moments.

It was, he decided, a baby possum. He had seen one once in Indian Guide camp, though it was larger than this.

He snapped off the flashlight, put it on the crate-table, and felt his way to the door.

—You take care of it till I get back—

—Yes—said the totem pole. —I'm used to animals—

The boy climbed down the tree and raced home.

The Great Door opened sternly.

The Great Lady pursed small lips.

The Great Gentleman made some remarks about birch switches and looked at the complicated computer/watch on his wrist.

The boy quivered, his eyes on his shoes. But he was thinking, *warm milk. How will I get it out there?*

At last, his bottom warmed by one didactic stroke from the birch switch, he was let go. His ears closed on sermons and an amen about going straight to bed.

He did go straight upstairs to his room. He stood still and listened for many minutes. Then he creaked down the back stairs.

No sign of Angelina. He had forgotten it was her night off!

His sister's doll house sat in a corner of the large kitchen. He found an eyedropper among the doll things. It took no time to pour a bit of milk into a pan and heat it. A jar with a screwtop held it. His jacket pocket held the jar.

He stood a moment, listening. Silence.

—You must say nothing—he said to the Great Back Door under the light.

And it didn't. It made no sound as the boy moved through it like a shadow, out into the night full of cricket-music and sycamore-speech.

Up, up the tree, into the House-That-Was-His-Own.

Groping, he found the flashlight, put the jar on the table, the eyedropper beside it.

Was the tiny creature still alive?

It was, was still pulsing, faintly but truly.

The boy slipped milk up into the dropper, put it ready on the crate-table. With a hand steady as a surgeon's he placed the possum in the palm of the other hand, then took up the dropper.

How miraculous that the small thing took a drop, then another, and another!

How miraculous that, after a long while, it curled its tail around his little finger and hung on like a miniature Mary Lou Retton. Swaying, swaying.

—Now we will go—said the totem pole—away into the Palace of the Forest—

So they did, the totem pole, the boy, the small possum clutching his finger.

Deep in the Palace they found a plump large possum wringing her paws. She was saying to a ring of opossums, "He was on my back; we were nipping along the tree branch at a great rate after I had found some delicious fruit, when the youngest slipped off. He fell away, away into a golden pool." She wiped her eyes. "I couldn't go down with all the others on my back, you see...."

At that moment the boy, the possum, and the totem pole walked into the ring of opossums who were shaking their heads.

Terrible to lose a child.

They jumped up at the sight of the trio, who marched like a small band, clapping hands, laughing.

There were no birch switches for the small latecomer. There were no sermons or final amens. There were huggings that squeezed almost to death, sweetmeats, and dancing in the greeny palace. Feathers fluttered like flags to make a weave on the floor full of color and light. Two owls lent the lamps of their eyes; there were cracklings and clatterings of joy. It was the jolliest place the boy had ever visited.

The lost-possum-who-had-come-home grinned from the safety of his mother's pouch. He watched the totem pole stomping gayly on its one leg, watched the boy's eyes glimmer and burn like just-lit candles in the jubilant dark.

•

"Here he is."

A rough voice slithered like a snake along the floor of the treehouse. "Here, sir. Here's your son." A policeman thrust himself through the narrow doorway.

"Bring him down. Bring him down immediately." It was the voice of the Great Gentleman. To the boy it sounded like swords clanging together.

"I'll do that, sir. You young hound, scaring your folks near to death." Rough hands grasped him, took him down to a quivering Great Gentleman, terrible in vivid rage.

"Do you not know it is Sunday morning? What do you mean by it, boy, running away, prostrating your mother?"

(What did prostrating mean? Had she developed a pouch he could crawl into?) He rubbed his eyes.

"Yes," the Great Gentleman shouted up the tree trunk. "Take an axe to it. Break it quite down. We'll have no more of this evil sneaking to darkness, this devilish hiding."

—But the possum—the boy's cry drowned in the deep waters of his throat.

At that moment it thumped at his feet.

Dead. Not playing possum.

Chopped pieces of the totem pole followed, the head dumb in the good Sabbath air.

—I remember what they said at Indian Guides—the boy half sobbed to the maple, wounded and weeping over him— at birth the baby opossum is no bigger than a kidney bean—

It wasn't much bigger now.

A *bean*—I will plant it. This is a magic bean and it will rise up into the Palace of the Great Forest—

He heard the Forest again, voices chattering, laughing, the clapping of many paws....

He continued to hear it, bent over, his bottom bare to the rod, the Great Gentleman sacrificing his son in the beautiful, sun-washed day.

—No bigger than a bean—the boy's voice was a whisper taken up by the robins like a thread they would work into the net of the Wild.

Blood dripped from the boy's whipped body like water, nourishing the planted seed.

The air clamored with the mystery of Sunday morning bells.

A Clutch of Feathers

Mr. Leamington had fed the ducks every day of his life since his retirement. Most days the boy, Lonny, joined him.

People in the park were used to them now. At first there was *talk*.

"That old man who lives in a shack and Lonny Clarke, the lawyer's son! He'd better be careful, that boy. The man's half crazy. He's apt to kidnap Lonny—or worse!"

Mr. Leamington never heard the talk, for nobody talked to him.

Lonny never heard it. His family lived on an isolated piece of land just outside town. Lonny's mother called it "the country place" as opposed to the city apartment. Lonny never had seen that. Lonny's father was too important and busy to be bothered with talk that his son spent all his free time with a strange old man.

His mother was as lovely as a piece of Doulton, and as untouchable. She crisply led all social events and rode to hounds in habits from London, erect and sleek as ice. She expected her well-paid housekeeper to keep six-year-old Lonny well mannered, well groomed, and well out of her way.

Anna was the only help they could get to live-in out of town. Anna was in love with Hank Draper, who rented out canoes, and spent every moment she could with him.

She knew Lonny spent his time with Mr. Leamington. She was delighted.

"Down on the lake, Hank can keep an eye on him."

Hank didn't.

Hank kept an eye on any woman who came to rent a canoe, and canoeing had become a popular pastime since brawny Hank, wide-smiled and drawling, had taken over the

business. Women came alone to canoe. They were so ignorant about boating techniques that Hank had to help them.
Of course.

It was early spring. Small bits of yellow fluff floated after
their mother through clouds on the lake.

"When they go under that bridge, away back where you
can't see them, can they see to follow their mother, Mr.
Leamington?" Lonny watched the mother and fluffs disappear.

"Beautifully." Mr. Leamington nodded his head, his long
white hair just like Merlin's in Lonny's picture book at home.
"You see, there is a lovely little house there, all golden, golder
than the ducklings, and lit by something brighter than the
sun."

"Brighter than the sun!" Lonny's eyes were harvest
moons.

"Oh yes." The nice thing about Mr. Leamington was the
way he was always sure about things. It gave you confidence.
"There is a little round lady who makes bread." Mr.
Leamington fingered the stale store-bought bread in his
pocket. "The little round lady loves animals, ducks, small
boys, and old men."

Lonny grinned; Mr. Leamington grinned back.

"There is a large fireplace in the big, cozy front room of
that house. The little round lady's husband keeps it going always. He sits beside it and plays games with anyone who wants
a turn."

"And doesn't he work all the time?" Lonny stared at the
black silent hole of the arched bridge. It really was a tunnel
that led to the next lake.

"No, only in the little garden beside the house. The boy,
the old man, and all the creatures help him plant it, and harvest it, and water it in summer."

"It's not true." Lonny's face was grave. "Ducks must have
water to live on. They cannot live in the warm cozy house or
work in the garden."

"They can," Mr. Leamington picked up a duck feather,

"for this is a magic house and garden. All things are possible. Anything you wish or imagine is possible in that house."

"Oh," Lonny clutched the old man's sleeve. "I want to go there. Can't we go and pay a visit?"

"Only the ducks are allowed to visit. Everyone else must stay forever—it's the way the magic works."

"I would *like* to stay forever. How can I go?"

"You must have a certain number of duck feathers. That's the entrance fee. Here's one for a starter, Lonny."

Lonny took the feather, white shading to deep brown. He turned it over in his hand and looked at it a long while.

How many will I need?" he asked, finally.

"Ah, they haven't told me that yet. All in good time, lad. Things can't be rushed when it comes to magic."

"Will you tell me as soon as you know?"

"I promise."

They watched the ducklings come out of the darkness into light. The boy and man shared some of the bread and threw some to the ducks. Then Lonny went home. Anna became very annoyed if he was late.

Summer came, a dry windless one. Lonny spent all day now with Mr. Leamington. His parents had gone to Europe. Anna spent her days with Hank, sometimes at the boathouse, away up the lake from where Mr. Leamington and Lonny watched the ducks, and sometimes at the big house, for who was there to see? Hank hired a high school boy to rent out canoes.

The ducklings grew large. Some died in the heat and lack of water. The lake was very low. Lonny watched some of the dead ducks drift under the weir bridge.

"Does the round lady bury them?" he asked Mr. Leamington.

"Bury them! Indeed not. She puts them in a little basket in front of the fire and warms them. Within a day they're as good as new and ready to swim again."

"Oh!" Lonny's face, so pinched by heat, almost smiled. "And those?" He pointed to some dead on the brown grass.

"The same, lad. The lady sends a special breeze that pulls

the inner part of them right into the basket. In there," Mr. Leamington pointed to the black arch, "they get a new body just like the old one, and off they go, flapping and quacking."

"But—" Lonny began.

Mr. Leamington stopped him, waggling a long thin finger. "Your trouble is, Lonny, that you don't really believe in magic. I told you, everything is possible. Here's another feather." It was a black one this time.

Lonny stuffed it deep in his pocket with the other. He didn't ask questions anymore. He knew Mr. Leamington would tell him when he had the proper number. And he knew they had to come from Mr. Leamington, who knew all about magic. Lonny couldn't just pick them up himself.

Slowly, he went home. The heat made him tired. There was only Anna's makeshift meal to look forward to anyway.

Hot summer lazed into autumn. Rains came. The lake's lapping sounded almost like clapping as it filled the cooling water. The trees, as if to make up for their wan summer appearance, bloomed leaf-brilliant reds, golds, browns. The ducks swam faster. There was no trace of dead ones. Of course Lonny knew where they were.

He sat with Mr. Leamington one brisk morning. Mr. Leamington frowned and seemed to be brooding about Lonny's last remark.

"This is the year you start in the school, Lonny, isn't it?" Mr. Leamington asked, surprised when the boy arrived as usual.

"No. Anna said my father made a killing." Mr. Leamington's eyesight was failing. He didn't see Lonny's look of fright or his shiver. "And was going to Swit-zer-land till after Christmas. And my mother has gone off with a prince." Lonny felt Mr. Leamington should understand that, knowledgeable as he was about magic.

So Mr. Leamington's frown surprised him.

As did his next remark.

"And Anna is under a spell, so she's no help." Mr. Leamington shook his white mane from side to side.

Anna under a spell! Lonny's listlessness disappeared for a moment. The magic was spreading!

Lonny said no more. Everything was possible, Mr. Leamington had said, and Mr. Leamington was the wisest person in the whole world.

Lonny came on and off all autumn. Whatever Anna's spell was, it kept her out overnight often. Sometimes she forgot to buy food. Lonny was often hungry. Occasionally he was so tired he slept very late and could not get himself to the lake.

He got there one December day, though. Ice covered the lake except for one end just in front of the weir bridge.

"The ducks are in open water, Mr. Leamington."

"Where are they, Lonny? Some days I don't see so well." The old man squinted through his ten-cent-store glasses.

"Right in front of the weir bridge. There's no ice there."

"Ah, you see, the warmth of the fire inside has glowed right out to protect them. That's the way it is with warmth."

"Last time I came there were colored leaves in the water."

"Mm...that was yesterday," Mr. Leamington nodded.

"No. Oh, no, I don't think so." Lonny was not quite sure himself.

"I forget things some days." Mr. Leamington got up and fumbled in his pocket for bread. "Let's go and feed them."

They walked to the open water, Lonny guiding his old friend.

"Last night I was in grade school," Mr. Leamington said, handing the boy a crust. "And there was Miss Watson upset at all the boys, same as always." Mr. Leamington laughed. The sound quavered into the lake.

Lonny didn't understand that at all. But if his friend said it, it must be so.

He tore up his crust and tossed the pieces to the ducks. They fought for them, gobbling them down in seconds.

"They were hungry," Lonny said, his own stomach in a knot.

"Yes. In summer they eat to be sociable, but in winter the masks are off."

Lonny stared at the ducks. Then—

"Look, look!" Lonny tugged at the old man.

"What is it, Lonny?"

"They're flying right up over the bridge. Over the trees, too," Lonny's eyes followed the flutter.

"They'll be back, don't worry. This is their home. Things always come home."

Lonny looked at his friend, who peered into the sky, not seeing.

Would his father come home then? And his beautiful mother? And Anna?

"I must go home," Lonny said.

The old man just nodded, cold wind riffling his silver hair.

Mr. Leamington was not much help to the policeman who questioned him two weeks later.

"Yes, he fed the ducks with me—yesterday? I think it was yesterday. I'm not sure anymore. Sick? Lonny? Homesick, mebbe. Not any other kind of sick that I know of. May I go to see him?" He tried to ignore the sharp pain inside him. He couldn't show *them.*

The policeman told him where Lonny was. After making marks in their black books, they went off.

It was awfully dark. Mr. Leamington could just barely see the outline of a boy lying surrounded by beautiful cerise velvet and flowers.

He managed to make out where a hand was. Before the attendant could stop him, he thrust a handful of duck feathers beside it. His own hand was as steady as his voice.

"There. You have enough feathers now, Lonny."

"Get that crazy old man out of here," a voice like ice on the lake hissed from the front row.

Mr. Leamington squinted at the Doulton figurine as he was being hustled out.

Not all the magic in the world could ever turn her into a little round woman who baked homemade bread.

•

Mr. Leamington had not gone to the cemetery, of course. They hurried him out of the funeral parlor. Strong-armed him. Most politely. One couldn't disturb other mourners.

Wind whipped, stung as if a giant cat-o'-nine-tails were being wielded. Mr. Leamington, eyes rheumy, blurred with cold, not tears, wandered slowly to the creek. He settled himself on a broken-down bench near the weir bridge. He hadn't a crumb, for himself or for the few ducks that huddled in a small patch of un-iced water. He leaned down to pick up one white straggly feather. He had no gloves. Soon his hands numbed so he couldn't hold the feather.

It fluttered back to the ground. A fierce blast of wind lifted it, suddenly; it twisted, twisted in air before dropping into the open tiny circle of water.

Mr. Leamington couldn't see it. He slumped on the rude bench, an old, cold, homeless man beyond magic, or any idea of magic.

Woman in a Special House

White birds come often to this beach where my small house holds its own far back from the water. Three of the birds are familiar, with a certain distinction about them. That is not to say I could with confidence call them gulls or terns. They're more exotic than either. They make a murmuring noise, though they are not roosting.

This morning I am dancing. One bird has flown off towards the brilliantly russet sun. I am inspired to try *Swan Lake*. I put on the cassette of the Philadelphia Orchestra under Ricardo Muti's direction. Muti is enchanting in that intense Italian way. And he's masterful with Russian music.

I find an old costume belonging to my sister. She's married and lives in California now. The feathers are bedraggled and bits of them whirl off as I dance, but what matter? My partner is Diaghilev in his heyday. There's never been any dancer like Diaghilev, *I* think. Stern and innovative, stunningly agile, marvelous looking. I am sure he always kissed ladies' hands.

After our pas de deux I sit down to rest, am shadowed a moment by one of the birds. It eases away and I think about Tschaikowsky and Von Meck. All those years of correspondence. How unsatisfying. But look what they produced. If I were not ever to offer my body to Charles again, would I produce anything for the ages? Would he?

Where *is* Charles, anyway? Is he annoyed because he likes lakes, not ocean? This comes up every summer.

"What about a little place at the ocean, Charles, this year? There's the boardwalk, evenings, and I love to fight the breakers, love to try to get out beyond them where there are just great swells."

"God save me from boardwalks." Charles holds his head. "For a woman of culture you have feet of clay."

I don't bother to straighten *that* out, for he gets annoyed if I nit-pick about English.

So, one year we go to the lake and one year to the ocean. I have to admit, except for the water (I hate lake water, all those strange, slimy, weedy things under the surface), Charles is right. The boardwalk, all boardwalks, are insults. We take a place at a beach without any boardwalk, finally, and just occasionally drive to the next town, with boardwalk, if we feel desperate enough to want grinding noise, deafening music, shuffling people, salt-water taffy machines, and the oddest tee-shirts I've ever seen.

"We might as well always go to the lake, Laura, where there is peace, quiet, and stars that come and sit on your shoulders."

"Mm—yes," I say, pulling at my lip. I love those things. But once in a while I like to slum and not have to drive one hundred miles to the nearest movie. Too, one simply mustn't give in so easily. A woman must take stands, must hang on to certain things as if they were life preservers, which in fact they may be.

So I don't really mean the "yes." Charles knows that, surely he does.

Here there is the immense ocean with its swells you can lie on, dream on. I forget Tschaikowsky, his homosexual anguish, and race to the shore, push past the breakers, and let myself go on one grand swell. How lovely, how bodiless I am, how otherworldly.

There is a white bird over me, again. It is dipping very near. It is immense. I am frightened. I cry out. It backs off. It is staring at me; it stares for a long, long time. I do not like its sharp purplish eyes.

What does it want of me?

I run back to my house, my feet ice cold, even on the burning sand. I sit in a corner of the living room and pull the Swan Lake costume over my eyes.

But you can't hide behind a costume forever. The bird is

nowhere in sight now, I see, inching from behind the ragged tutu. I am alone in this house; it is very cold.

I want Charles. We have been married ten years. We have no children, can't have them. We've decided to adopt. We've already started negotiations for a Colombian boy and girl. I am thrilled, more, I am deeply satisfied in some center of myself. We will bring them to the shore. Charles will make one of the sandcastles he builds as if he were creating one of the great chateaux of France. Or Buckingham Palace, maybe. He takes endless pains and time. People come to look at his work, astonished. It is the one thing about the beach that he adores.

"A pity the tide will wash it all away," I am always moved to comment.

"The fun is in the making of it." Charles smiles in his easy way. The sun has made his faun-colored hair almost blond. Normally angular, he has put on rounding pounds in our lolling, swimming, eating, reading, lazy vacation life.

Yes, he will make our children wonderful castles. We will all walk and gather shells. We will explain to them, carefully, what each one is. We always bring with us books on birds, shells, trees, frustrated if we can't know what the world is about.

I sit at the window of my house, across which straggles a vine-like weed, like veins across my eyes. I don't recognize the weed and am about to get the book when the bird comes back with another bird. I haven't seen this one before; it has feathers green as jade. I shudder, afraid, as they come close to me.

Then I see.

I see what they are.

"It's been six months, doctor. Nothing. Not a flicker. Not even when her husband comes in."

Not even when her husband comes in.

"No, no," I shout. "Charles hasn't come. I keep wondering where he is."

"A little tremor of her left hand, that's all," the green birdman says, bending over me. "A terrible thing. Beautiful young woman, everything to live for. Hope they jail the guy that hit her in that alley, for a long, long time."

"What are you talking about? Tell me, tell me. Charles, where are you?"

"Trouble is, they're out of jail in no time, these days." My white nursebird tucks covers round my feet. "Do you suppose the family will petition to take her off the respirator, doctor, eventually?"

God. My God. I am *alive.*

"Much too soon even to think about that, nurse, though in this case...it tears you apart, no matter how often you see it."

"Yes, sure does." The white bird raises one wing to a bottle over my head.

"Listen," I scream. "*I can hear you.* Can't you hear me? Listen, please listen."

"The hand tremor has stopped. Just keep her as comfortable as possible, nurse, though she can't feel anything."

"You're wrong, terribly wrong." I have never shrilled so loud before in my life. "This morning I felt my feet dancing; it was quite wonderful. I was listening to Tschaikowsky, was thinking about how many years he wrote to Von Meck. *Listen.* I was swimming, was gathering shells, was waiting for Charles, thinking about being in bed with him...."

The nursebird comes to adjust the dinosaur that puffs beside me.

"Have you children?" I shriek. "A husband? Don't you understand...."

She flies away.

I know now that I must hoard all energy, all thought, towards plotting how to get out.

This is just a house. I must batter down these doors, break these windows, tear away all weeds. The thin wisp of my breath, so like a silken thread that tethers me to Charles, to Muti, to Diaghilev, to my children, must go on.

Enormous black clouds of wild, wild birds beat in me, pecking, scratching, squawking. Summoning great sharp whips from the storehouse of me, I bat them away. I must bang, kick, fist at the doors, the windows. Houses can be broken, even the sturdiest.

I cannot yet get to the ocean, cannot get past the breakers to the lovely mauve-azure buoyant water that would hold me, to the swells that would carry me lightly, lightly, everywhere, anywhere.

No. Not yet. But I can hear, beyond the crashing, foaming breakers, the sounds in the falling swells. Fish turn, lazily, lithely, in silvery bodies, telling old tales. Seaweeds amble to, fro, to, fro, full of syllables retrieved from the shores they've touched. Shells tumble on deep sands like children somersaulting, cartwheeling; they murmur and laugh. Crabs, lobsters tell me of ancient places, remarkable waters.

I am not alone in this house.

All creatures and things of the sea whisper, whisper, their long poems of survival.

I am in touch with whatever I need to swim, strongly.

Soon the white birds and the green birds will wear the silken shawls I have made for them, of my ongoing breath.

They will understand that they are prayer-shawls they must not discard.

Listen, you can hear me weaving from the depths of the earliest seas.

In a moment, this very moment, I am going to dance again. This time to the immense important swells of *La Mer.*

The Last One on Earth

It is at night that I dream. Or is it just memory swaying its old dances? Are memories dreams? Are dreams memories?

I have nothing but time, now, to think about these things. Little time, I suppose. My bones creak at the slightest turn; I am ragged, and, yes, unkempt. This heat bothers me. I am weighted down by it. Strange that something one cannot see is so heavy. This afternoon while the sun still rode high on its avenues of blue and changing white shapes, a leaf, orange and scarlet, flew in the window someone had opened, and settled on the floor. I knew, then, that a change in the weather must be near, even though my breath steams in my throat.

There are stars tonight. I see them quite clearly. Well, clearly as rheumy eyes allow. I remember them above a wood rich with birch and oak. I can still smell the wood's dank musk, that inviting scent that lured us in. I cannot now crack acorns as I did then, gorging myself on a banquet of nuts. As we all did. If there had been a pool, I imagine I would have laughed at my reflection, my crop so stuffed I could barely move to the alder swamp where we sat, the trees so weighted with us that we looked, from a distance, like strangely misplaced haystacks. So one of us, arriving late, said.

But I was talking about stars, those friends that guided us through our lives, brilliant chips scattered across sometimes moonless heavens. We never understood them. Were they another species too high ever to need to roost? Did they mate to reproduce their brilliance? In what fields, swamps, or trees did they eat? *What* did they eat? The blue fields of night offered them nothing but themselves, and sometimes the ball of moon, itself a mysterious creature, thinning, fattening before our eyes. And when the largest creature of all reared out of the sea to ride on daylight's pale highways, had it eaten the stars? That creature, in some half frightening, half wonderful way, *was* daylight.

Huddling together, we whispered about these things. In a lifetime I have found no answers. I know only that they were friendly to us, if distant. They seemed to have no speech, or if they did, they were too far for us to hear.

He said I was beautiful. And I was, you know. I saw myself in the cold lake water of a northern place. My eyes were a hot orange-red (Oh, I learned to flick them at males). I thought the bluish slate of my head stylish, the metallic luster of my shoulders and neck sensuous. I preened on a branch hanging over the lake, perfecting myself for what other women whispered to me was better than rocketing towards the sky.

It was in April that we met, that sweet fecund month. We sang, loosing on soft winds a bell-like call, clear as spring water. Or, I thought, like the tinkling of bells heard on the horse-drawn sleighs we often swept over in wintertime.

Scrub oaks ahead of us scratched the sky. I knew that was the stand where I must shine for the handsome one I'd decided must be mine. I flashed through the branches, displaying (shamelessly!) my remarkable ability to maneuver. I laughed as I dipped, swerved, swung towards the sky, whirling at the line of suitors on my trail, among them (looking distraught!) the one I wanted. "So demure," I'd heard some of them whisper, miles back. Well, they knew now there was more than that to my beauty.

At last I decided I'd teased them enough. Besides, the game was wearing. I found a branch set like a throne above the ground where panting males engaged in a scrambling battle. For me! How heady it is to be young and beautiful. The battle was frightening, though. They thrashed terribly, stabbed at each other. I caught my breath. Then, relieved, I saw they didn't stab at eyes, just at each other's bodies. Bad enough, but at least not blinding. And it was, withal, fascinating!

I don't know how long I sat, proud, tremulous, before,

one by one, they were vanquished. It was thrilling to see, in my chosen one's mouth, a tuft of feathers from one older man who'd had enough! And to see, even far above, a furious fire burning in my would-be lover's eyes. How strong he was. I quivered with longing. Listen! All this time later I can still hear the deep soft cooing of him, can still see the fluff of his iridescent robes as he followed me, I suddenly timorous, from ground to bush to tree to ground. Then the sweet, mad, long kiss, his beak in my mouth, until, lost, I opened my wings to him, my young lithe body yawning wide for his rocking me to heights never known before. Oh, the frenzied ache of the taking.

Even old, you remember the moment when the world crazily swirled.

If only I could, now, ever rest so totally as after that heady explosion of light, I would thank all the winds of the world, those winds for so long the gods of my life.

A step on the gravel path. Is someone coming to take me somewhere else? For I don't want to go anywhere else, as I so passionately did for so long.

No. Whoever, whatever it was has gone. The sound stirred me to other time, to the turnings and turnings of seasons when I used to hear the thunderous beating of millions of wings. We darkened the world with our fluttering blanket!

"An eclipse," I heard a small boy shout, once, as we thundered overhead, and saw him dive for his mother's skirts. Curious, I watched, saw him recover. He rushed to join the crowd of men and boys who lined the river road. I wanted, the first year, to dip down, perch on the small boy's shoulder, to tell him we meant no harm, that I would play with him if he wanted, for a while. I was soon set straight.

"Fool. That is a fearful species called man. They live only to kill us. See those things in their hands shooting fire? Stay as high as you can. Never, never go near them."

All these years I've never understood it. What about us made them hate us so? Why did they laugh while they spilled out their fire? I never told the rest, but sometimes I used to sit on a twig above the river, far from the ravenous crowd, and look at my reflection. And saw nothing anyone might fear. I'd lift one foot, then the other, scrutinize my claws, which could never hurt the gigantic beasts who felled us, felled us incessantly, endlessly. A mystery. Why? What did they do with the great bags of us they gleefully toted off when evening began its welcome darkening?

It is the birches I remember most vividly, the lovely, tall, spindly birches where we loved to nest. I remember the sound of the wind through them at night, mixed with the soft murmur of squabs before sleep.

And before the thump, thump of long poles against trunks roused us, stunned, from the sweet haven.

It was the beasts, hitting, hitting, knocking some nests loose, squabs and young flying into the air before falling to earth.

They were never satisfied, the strange, fierce, two-legged beasts. They wanted us all.

The beautiful bark on the tree, thin as the paper we saw sometimes blowing across fields, was always peeling, in an ancient wisdom that knew the old must always make way for the new.

One of the beasts would take out a little stick which suddenly flamed. He'd touch it to the bark at the base of our airy homes.

Still, I can see the flash, the instant fire racing to every inch of the tree, bathing it in a fierce flame.

I was lucky; I got away, but I saw friends, plumage badly scorched, cartwheel to the ground, while nests burned, burned.

In minutes the trees we loved turned into halls of flaring horror.

They'd bag fifty of us at a time. From just one birch.

They ignited *all* the birches they could see.

The question pounds in my head again tonight, remembering: *What did they do with the great bags of us?*

These long years later, my eyes blur with those flames, and tears.

•

It is the loneliness now that stuns me day and night. There was an old man with me for a while, not one I ever knew in my youth. Not my love, not like my love at all, but a good companion. He perched close to me, so close we knew the beatings of each other's heart. The old need that, need to know near them the tick that speaks life, need to know their own kind is close by, hearing the same old echoes in the head. Huddled close we saw the same luscious stands of trees we saw as we soared, millions of us, from the warm south to cooler expanses, sensed the same dangers, the same exquisite small joys, and shared, unspoken, the same dreams, memories.

I don't know how long it has been since he died, the dear old one who made time's hollow reverberations bearable, but I watched him grow frailer and frailer, unable to help, knowing myself fading too.

How the reverberations shake my cage, rattle in every corner. *We were the beautiful passengers,* voices whisper, and I strain to see them again, hurtling through the heavens at great speed, strain to hear the beating music of uncountable wings, among them my own, battering back the night.

The old creature, sun, moves on his radiant hooves again. I turn in my cage towards him. But he brings me no warmth today. Even the echoes fade to a place I can no longer reach.

Was it all ever real? I wonder, for I know the old are confused and imagine things that never were. Am I poised in a dream I only imagine is memory?

There is no answer. Only a silence.

Terrible.

Endless.

Note: The last passenger pigeon died September 1, 1914, at the age of twenty-nine.

Journal

Sometime I may have children. What will they think of me, whom they will know only as mother, never as child, girl, lover, teacher, the other things I am?

I keep this journal about you, Mama. One day I will give it to you and you may read how I see, saw, you, for I believe you are as curious as I about the multiple personalities we are. Eves, all of us, with many faces, fading from one to another like special effects no camera records.

This is sporadic, erratic, nothing disciplined about it, written at random when emotion dictates, or need.

Shame.

I am ashamed of you. It is summer and you are in your room looking out on the tree-brimmed street, reading, of course. I always think of you reading. It is just after supper and humid beyond bearing. I am fifteen. My god is "what others think." I look at you, damp and contented, lost in your other world. Why, why is there a dirty rim around the collar of your cotton dress? Having worked in it all day, why didn't you change if for dinner? Oh yes, I noticed it at dinner, the ten of us hungry as loosed hibernators.

I see the old, imperfect kitchen, the fey black oven that lights only upon incantation, with a great frightening pouf; see the icebox that is less than competent. More clearly, I see the grey depressed rim of the sweaty dress as I gobble your goodness. Why do you not look like the movie stars I see at the Saturday afternoon movie? Why, dinner done, have you still not changed?

I do not understand. I do not understand the old iron set up in your bedroom, the chair beside it piled with washed clothes. I am angry. You could, at least—my mind slips to the earlier irritation—*wash*.

It is early morning. You are playing the piano. You play splendidly, poignantly. Why not, your alma mater the London College of Music?

"But where is the blue skirt I must wear to school today?"

Your music breaks off. Apologetically, you run to that pile in your bedroom, unearth the skirt, and transform it to smooth. You bring it to me, in my slip combing my hair. It *will* not go in the right direction.

"How could you have forgotten it?" I scold.

"I'm sorry," you smile. "Shall I start your breakfast now?"

"In five minutes." I am distracted by a red something on my chin.

"You're so pretty, an anemone."

I frown. I barely hear you.

"That Irish family with all the dirty children."

I am going up the steps to my house after school. They think I cannot hear them, three popular Helens of our class. I want to cry; I want to kill them; I want to kill you.

Eight children. How could *anyone* have eight children? It is obscene. It is dirty, as we often are. Why are you so busy reading or playing the piano that you do not see that we are *always* clean, our clothes always immaculate?

When I go in you are playing Bach. I hate Bach. I clatter down my books in the cluttered living room. Why haven't you cleaned it? Not a chair not piled with music or books. *Not a chair not piled with music or books,* I scream at you. Your music stops. I am glad I can stop your music, your reading. Why should you live in those worlds when we are in *need*?

You are in the garden. You are talking to plants, years before anyone heard of talking to plants. Your garden is eloquent, but your hands are dirty, so dirty. And where is the white blouse I *must* have for my date tonight? You drop spade and wash—both hands and blouse—and press it. I do not question that you wait on me. You are my mother; it is your *privilege*.

•

I am twenty-two. We could not afford college for me. I work in an office. I feel like a misfit. These people have read nothing. I wander Hardy's country, or Little Gidding.

"You're a regular Cassandra," I shake my head at a co-worker.

She looks at me, blankly. Should she be angry or glad? Have I insulted or praised?

I am bewildered. Where are people who have read anything? I see you reading to me each night, see myself picking up one of your books, dropped carelessly everywhere, see myself curled in its intricacies, from seven years to the present....

I am auditioning. I sing Bach. Well. I know it as I know my name. Yes, I am accepted for this prestigious chorus. I hear your endless Bach that I cut off for my endless necessities....

A date takes me to his home, a great estate with fine gardens.

"Lobelia," I exclaim, "lupine, oh the primroses."

"What queer things you know." He mixes a cocktail.

I want the tang of the garden, its wild ways....

I want to give you this journal, you with your love of the written word, of learning, however haphazardly perused. I take it to your room, in the middle of the night. This odd urgency.

You are not there. I knew that. I heard them carry you out this morning, the solemn feet of undertakers walking through snatched sleep. I am happy that you are not here, for you were in great pain, for a long time.

I am happy that, when you could no longer see, I read you the journal, happy that we laughed and cried together over it, happy that I heard you angrily refute imprecise perceptions. I am happy I had the courage to share it with you, that I was able to show you sides of you that you might not have known, happy that I could thank you for great books and music and simple and splendid flowers.

I place it on your bedside table beside a glass of daisies.

Margaret, my mother.

I go to the window and look at the sky, starless and blank, blank as the blank white pages you will never read, that I have never written.

I am nude in my lie, in the make-believe I have almost believed.

The moon shows a silver, slim light, arriving too late.

The Desert Shall Rejoice

Christmas and home are synonymous in her mind. Theirs was a Christmas straight out of Dickens, a wonderful, sparkling event in their lives. In retrospect it is their loveliest family remembrance. They look back on it as the perfect time, they who can never share it again. Though they may share Christmas now with their children, those Christmases, with Mama as their center, are in the shimmering wonderland of long-ago-and-never-again.

They were a very close family, their mother's sister, (beloved Ninny, who had always lived with them), Peg's three sisters and two brothers, all now married and away from home, her father and she, the youngest of the six children. They used to pity families with only one or two children. How *dead* those homes must be! Their household was a tremendous hive of bustling activity towards December 25. Oh, the trimming, wrapping, cooking, writing and receiving of cards, the playing of timeless Christmas music on the piano, Mama's expert fingers leading them all. Mama, a graduate of the London College of Music, had never let her music slip, six children and the active life of a minister's wife notwithstanding.

Buying for Christmas 1949 had been such fun! Mama and Peg had gone shopping gayly, through crowds and dancing snow. With what delight they found a record of "The Teddybears' Picnic," first popular that year and the perfect gift for several of Mama's fourteen grandchildren. Eight of the fourteen grandchildren were with them that year, in addition to the nine core family members, plus Peg's sisters' and brothers' respective husbands and wives. As for so many years before, Mama and their father, Dada, unobtrusively directed activities, and they all were children, still. After dinner, music *was* the house, part of the walls, the rugs, the old battered furniture, the kettle poised on the stove for tea, the dog's ancient bones, the cat's orange fur, her wary green eyes. Mama was at the piano, Dada played the violin, and all sang in parts, as they had been trained to do as small children barely able to walk.

The only shadow cast on the festivities was that Mama had a very slight, ever-present earache, but she rarely spoke of it and never let it stop her enjoyment. The family, callous as people often are about someone else's slight sickness, paid as little attention to it as she apparently did.

Too soon that wonderful Yule season was over. Family members again took up their separate lives in widely scattered cities, leaving Mama, Ninny, and Peg to carry on with the dull routine of January, always a "let-down" month. Dada, a Home Missionary for the Board of Home Missions in New York, went off on a month's trip through Indiana.

The earache which had bothered Mama through the holiday season, still, in the middle of January, remained. Their friendly general practitioner, who had given Mama several treatments for an ear infection, told Peg one day, quite casually, that since the earache was still there, he'd like Mama to see a specialist. So, cheerily, she went off to Dr. Williams, laughing aside Peg's suggestion that she accompany her. At dinner that evening Mama told Ninny and Peg, in her calm way, that her earache was slightly worse because Dr. Williams had taken a small piece from inside the ear to put through analysis.

"'Just routine,' he says," she told them, and Ninny and Peg, ignorant of the medical world and its workings, for they were singularly free of illness in their family, accepted the statement and tucked Mama into bed at an early hour, a heating pad on the offending ear.

At work the next day Peg's brother phoned her, told her that Dr. Williams had called him and advised him that Mama had a serious mastoidal condition and must have an operation at once. Dr. Williams, Trevor told Peg, was making immediate arrangements for Mama's entrance into hospital.

They would operate two days following at 2:00 P.M.

Peg put down the receiver, only half believing. It had been so abrupt a statement; she had been so totally unprepared for it. Mama seriously ill? Mama, who in her small person embodied immeasurable moral strength for them all, and, indeed, physical strength as well. One of Peg's mental pictures of her is the sight of Mama effortlessly moving her beloved piano around the drawing room alone. Surely Trevor was mistaken, had somehow misunderstood Dr. Williams.

But it was, after all, terribly true. That evening they drove Mama to the hospital. All of them, particularly Mama herself, made brave remarks about how fine it would be when this was all over and she would be home, quite well, planting, with her usual joy and enthusiasm, her spring garden. Why, mastoids are nothing these days, they all assured one another, fear lying like some grey ghost on their hearts as, inevitably, Ninny and Peg had to leave her, looking so game and cheery, so small and defenseless in the stark hospital bed, for the night.

Dada arrived home the next morning, having been summoned by Trevor. After forty years together they were not to be separated in this unbelievable crisis. Dada, true to character, covered up his terrible fear and bewilderment with his usual blustering, histrionic manner, but Mama was glad to have him home. Of course she didn't say as much. They were of the outwardly undemonstrative Victorian era, but their very casualness and brusqueness told you they were lovers still.

Having installed a television set in Mama's room, to which she consented, Peg felt sure, more to please the family than because she wanted it (Mama was addicted to *books*), they had to leave. There were many preparations the staff had to make for the next day's operation.

Peg went to work the following day. There are times when work is the most wonderful pain-killer in the world. Gratefully she cleaned out files, brought up to date certain records—jobs she had been putting off for weeks. At 2:00 P.M. her mind flew to the hospital. The thought of her kind, gentle, loving mother going under the surgeon's knife was a nightmare to her. It seemed an unutterably lonely experience. They who loved her so much could not be with her, could not help her. She was among stark white strangers. Would they be kind? Peg tried to continue working at the furious pace she had set herself that morning but could not keep her mind off the scene centered around an operating table where her mother, her dear Mama, was, for once in her shy retiring life, the center of attention.

Peg phoned home several times during the next two hours, but there was no word. Mama was still in the operating room. When Peg arrived home at 5:00 she learned that Mama had only just come out of the operating room, at 4:30. Two and one half hours! It was apparently a more complicated operation than any of them had suspected.

The next morning they went to see Mama. The gallant little figure, head swathed in bandages, brought tears to their eyes. But Mama was as calm, kind, optimistic, and interested as always. She wanted to know all that had been happening. Had they played canasta last night? Had Dada rested enough after his trip? Was Peg's cold better? No thought for herself, but only for them. This was the essence of Mama.

She seemed so well! They called Dr. Williams, thanked him for performing such a fine operation. If his reply was guarded, they did not notice in the excitement of knowing that Mama was all right, was coming *home.*

In only two days she *was* home, head still almost completely covered with bandages, of course, but what matter, she was home. The strangely silent, waiting house awakened, seemed to dance with light.

It was a week later at luncheon on Sunday that Peg noticed that one side of Mama's mouth had dropped, giving her face a twisted, crooked look. Peg mentioned it to Ninny later. Ninny said yes, she had noticed, but of course had said nothing to Mama. Dada was too wrapped up in his job of "getting Mama better," which consisted largely of forcing her to eat things she did not want but which she gamely struggled to down, a daily ritual which irritated Peg almost beyond bearing, to notice the sadly drooping mouth. Ninny and Peg discussed it, decided that probably with the healing of the wound the mouth would come back into proper shape. Nevertheless, they made note to ask Dr. Williams about it on Mama's next visit to him.

Peg went about her daily secretarial job with a lighter heart than she had had in weeks. Mama's convalescence seemed slow, but it was of no moment as long as she was home and they could care for her and could, unconsciously, draw strength from her. Mastoidal operation patients, Dr. Williams had told them, always made a slow recovery. This they in turn told Mama when she, rarely and hesitatingly, as if she were afraid of bothering them, asked if they thought she was making progress.

So Peg was surprised one day when her brother Trevor came on a rare visit to her office, said he would like to talk to her about Mama. Of course, she said, offering him a chair. *What was there to talk about?* Trevor went right to the point. Dr. Williams had called him to his office, had told him the entire facts of Mama's case. She had cancer of the ear. When he operated he found it had already spread too far. Mama had about six months to live.

Peg has no recollection of Trevor's leaving. She does not remember working that afternoon. She does vividly remember a series of flashbacks which her mind presented. Whether it was for a moment or an hour she does not know. In retrospect she spent what seemed like the whole afternoon. A hundred pictures of Mama came to mind. Mama teaching her early piano essentials; Mama joyously playing hymns on Sunday morning, their first sound on that Sabbath day. Mama buying her a pair of gay red pyjamas one Christmas because she especially wanted them. Knowing Peg's love of the cat, Mama waking her in the morning with a cheery "The cat's back, ducky," after one of kitty's three- or four-day jaunts somewhere. Mama, possessor of the original emerald thumb, happily taking a slip of some plant she particularly wanted from the arboretum.

"Of course it's not stealing," she would indignantly insist when one of them pointed out that this practice probably was frowned upon in the best arboretum circles. "Plants and trees belong to God."

And their dear Mama, scrupulously honest in every detail, could never be brought to see that some officials really are stuffy about this sort of thing!

Mama, who stayed on at the failing downtown church as organist long years after Peg's father had left it as pastor, trailing down to it, an hour's journey each way by streetcar on Sunday morning, often wheezing with the asthma which plagued her in winter. In vain did they plead with her to give it up. Uselessly they pointed out that for the four or five old people still attending, some neighborhood pianist would do. Their insistence that she at least not give back in the collection the entire small salary they paid her fell on deaf ears. "It's my duty," said Mama, and that was that. Duty to Mama was as the Rock of Gibraltar. Nothing they could say to this gentlest of women could budge her.

Mama's music was the theme which ran through all Peg's reminiscences. She could read any piece of music, play anything by ear, transpose anything into any key. As Peg made an effort to start to type that long, long afternoon, she could see Mama wistfully, beautifully, playing the old lovely Irish airs she knew so well and loved so deeply. Peg used to think that in this music Mama went back again to girlhood days in Ireland, carefree golden days when she had been, as their grandmother had often told them, "the belle of the county." Mama's later life had not been easy, though it had been happy. Used to the best of everything and to being "county," it had, Peg was sure, been hard for her to become used to the rigid life of a minister's wife, with six small mouths to feed on a less-than-slim budget. So Peg felt that music was her release, that in its mystical, mythical realms she lost herself and dreamed dreams of the green island she loved and was never able to revisit.

The day of Trevor's visit ended, unbelievably. Peg went home to dinner, not knowing how she could face Mama, how she could keep her from seeing the anguish that filled heart and mind. But some Being gives strength. Peg remembers with crystal clarity that she told a number of gay stories at dinner, even one which made Mama laugh. A few moments later she could have cut her throat, gladly, for apparently that small excitement was more than Mama could stand. She had to throw up, there at the dinner table. She apologized abjectly, oh so abjectly, for upsetting their dinner, thinking of them again, not of herself and the terrible pain that bout of illness caused her. Peg left the table, went to her room, where, lacking Mama's great courage, she lay on her bed and cried, cried.... At length she slid to her knees and prayed an unbelievable prayer: that God would take Mama from them soon and end her hideous, unaidable suffering. Bitterly, Peg felt that was the least He could do.

Incurable cancer follows a pattern, as anyone who has had it in the family knows. The patient is given dope to alleviate pain, and progressively more dope as an immunity to the earlier amount builds up. Dr. Williams started Mama with large white pills. Today Peg can sketch their size accurately. They gave Mama so many, so frequently. When each one was just about wearing off, Mama's pain, ever constant but dulled by the pill, would start to come to the fore before the next pill they had given her took effect.

Every other day one of them drove Mama the three miles to Dr. Williams' office, where he rebandaged the wound. Mama and Dr. Williams became close friends. Mama was so gallant, so radiantly good, so uncomplaining in the face of what must have been almost unbearable pain. Dr. Williams had in his waiting room all manner of beautifully blooming plants, some very rare. Through all her agony Mama's life-long love of anything growing asserted itself. She and Dr. Williams exchanged slips and plant lore along with bandages.

Those trips to his office were, however, nightmares. Every bump, though slight, was as a searing knife in Mama's head. They crawled down the busy thoroughfares so as not to jar her, but this gave impatient unknowing drivers an opportunity to lie on their horns. Their blasts echoed through poor Mama's head, and it was heart-rending to see her agony and be helpless in the face of it. Upon arrival at Dr. Williams' office she was done in and would have to have a hypodermic needle before he could work on her. Shortly the insistent, jabbing, relentless pain would settle to a dull ache, and she would be interestedly chatting with her friend and doctor about his plants.

After the large white pills came very small white ones. Soon these were of no value taken orally and she was then put upon hypodermic needles full time. At first, having had some experience with giving herself needles for asthma, she took this chore upon herself. The day soon came when she was too weak to do this. Peg took over the job. She can never describe and will never forget what it cost her to jab poor Mama's leg or arm, each already dotted with angry red specks from the hated, yet wonderful, needle. But what it cost Peg was as nothing to what Mama was going through. Just before the needle Ninny or Peg would often come on her, her head in her hands, crying softly to herself, "Oh, what shall I do, what shall I do?" Then, as she saw them, she would become very quiet, would patiently wait until Peg had given her the blessed needle. How many times in the night Ninny or Peg rose to prepare and administer the hypodermic, for Ninny soon learned how to give it. The procedure was to dissolve one little white pill in a teaspoon of water over a small old oil lamp they had rigged up outside Mama's door. Then carefully, very carefully, so that no air got in, they sucked this solution up into the needle. Peg cannot begin to tell anyone what Ninny was to Mama during that terrible six months. Ninny's labor was a labor of love indeed. She quite literally wore herself out in caring tenderly, lovingly, unceasingly, for Mama. She was with her all day and often all night. No task was too menial or too great if it would help Mama. She was her sister's keeper.

But everyone was good to Mama. It was easy to be; she had spent her life being kind and good to them. How little it was, really, for Peg's married sisters to arrange their own homes and lives so that they could come and spend a week or so, alternatingly, helping to care for Mama.

Peg wonders if, during their moments with Mama, they

have any remembrances as bitter and unerasable as hers. There was the Sunday morning when Peg was alone with Mama. Ninny had gone to church, one of the rare occasions when she consented to leave her post of love and duty. None of Peg's sisters was then visiting. Mama's poor mouth was terribly dry, yet a drink of water always made her nauseous. She took out her false teeth, something dignified Mama would never do under ordinary circumstances, and asked Peg to run cold water over them and bring them back. Peg is stupidly fastidious about such things. She hates to touch other people's false teeth, hates the sight of blood, loathes cleaning up after someone has been ill. In short, it is small wonder that nursing has not been her chosen profession. When Mama handed out her teeth Peg hesitated, infinitesimally, but long enough for her dear sensitive mother to know what was going through her mind. There was no anger, no resentment. "Poor ducky," was all she said. "I know how you hate it, but it would be such a relief."

Peg can never forget that Sunday.

There was the evening Dada was hovering over Mama, forcing her to eat something she did not want and had already refused. Trying, as usual, to please, Mama finally consented to take a spoonful, although she knew full well, and they all knew, that it would immediately make her sick. That particular night it was more than Peg could stand. She screamed at him to let Mama alone. He, a highly sensitive man with a keen but wholly unstudied instinct for the dramatic, looked amazed for an instant, then went into the dining room, put his head down on his hands, and cried with sobs that seemed to tear his heart out, in between making statements to the effect that Peg was crucifying him.

She wanted to run wildly out into the night. To think that in trying to help Mama she had created this terrible scene, while Mama was dying. Was *dying*! It was more than Peg could bear. True to character, Mama herself was the peacemaker, soothing Dada and saying just the right things to Peg, never mentioning the fact that her pain was becoming unbearable, that needle time was imminent.

Peg never forgets these things; they remain crosses, burdens to bear, in silence and alone.

Often during those terrible months they read to Mama her favorite chapter from the Bible, the thirty-fifth chapter of Isaiah. Mama was a deeply religious woman—not volubly. Her religion was as simple as a child's. She believed in and lived by the principles of Christianity; with no fuss or strain, and with a good Irish sense of humor. Her religion was not a matter of conjecture or theologic debate. She *knew* that "sorrow and sighing shall flee away." They who loved her so much tried to comfort her in her solitary world of pain, but what could they offer that was worth even half what she found in the Book which had sustained her for some sixty years? When she became so weak and her eyes failed so that she could no longer read at all, they used to find, after a hypodermic had put her to sleep oh so temporarily, the Bible closed on her finger, marking this chapter of Isaiah.

It was about five months after Mama first became ill that they had to tell her that Dr. Williams had died, suddenly, of a heart attack. She said so little, only instructed them to send his favorite flowers, one of the plants they had discussed with such enthusiasm. Then she seemed to retire a little farther into herself and the great reservoirs of courage and understanding which were hers. Did she, in her infinite wisdom, know that she would so soon be joining him, that the parting from this good, kind friend was temporary, that they would meet again in a land covered with blossoms such as they had never known on earth?

For they had never told Mama that her time with them was limited. They had avoided all mention of her true illness and had been careful to tell her that the needles she was taking were to make her better, but that this was a long, arduous illness, slow to cure. This was the climate of silence about cancer in another time. In Peg's mind now she is sure they underestimated Mama. She had always been an unusually intelligent woman. Peg doesn't think they ever fooled her. She thinks Mama knew, and, thinking to save them any awkwardness or embarrassment or pain in having to speak of death, let them think she thought she was getting better. But gradually she prepared herself for what was to come next and, Peg thinks, tried to prepare her family. She prayed often, quietly, sincerely, simply, and with dignity.

Some of the family became daily more bitter towards God. Why had He singled out their mother, a saint indeed, whose whole life had been spent in His service, for this terrible unabating form of torture? But Mama never seemed to question, never blamed. It was as if she knew, somehow, the purpose of it all.

"Oh, Lord, help me to stand it," was all Peg ever heard her say, and that in moments of deepest agony, with tears running down her face so that Peg wanted to take her in her arms and comfort her, as she had so often comforted Peg.

Mama was rapidly becoming weaker. One day she climbed into bed, never to leave it again in this life. "Let me die in peace," she wrote on the back of an old envelope, almost illegibly, for she now could not see at all and could barely speak, the effort was so great.

The whole family came then, Peg's three sisters and two brothers, to join her, Ninny and Dada in constant vigil as they waited, dry-eyed, tear-drenched inside, for Mama to leave them. They took turns remaining by her bedside so that she would never be alone for a moment. It was so terribly, unspeakably lonely, this journey she had to take. They loved her so much; she was so dear to them, the motivating force in their close family circle, but in the end they could do nothing for her.

While Peg was by her side Mama woke once out of her state of coma and cried, pitifully, weakly, "Who is there?" Peg told her and Mama whispered, "Oh, Peg, Pegeen, my baby, you know I love you." And she held Pegeen for a moment strongly, for the last time, in her arms, then dropped back into unconsciousness while Peg, tears streaming down her face, gave Mama, following doctor's instructions, one last hypodermic in her leg, already cold and no longer Mama.

It was just towards dawn on July 1, 1950, that Dada called them into Mama's room and they saw Mama pass peacefully and as gently as she had done everything all her life from her world of agony into a world where "the eyes of the blind shall be opened, and the ears of the deaf shall be unstopped. The parched ground shall become a pool, and the thirsty land springs of water."

And the day broke, and the shadows flew away.